"THE PLOT KEEPS YOU GOING RIGHT ALONG."
The New York Times

He didn't feel like a murderer. Hell—he didn't feel at all. And if what he did was inhuman, it was just too bad for humanity.

Tom was rich, spoiled, glib—and handsome enough to have any woman he wanted, even Ellen Case. But even Tom couldn't be that inhuman—not without paying a shattering price!

"Terse, exciting, stimulating . . . written with an almost cruel economy."
The Buffalo Evening News

"Sticks in the reader's mind."
The Hartford Times

"Haunting, fascinating . . . beautifully controlled."
The Boston Herald

Running Scared

GREGORY MCDONALD

AVON
PUBLISHERS OF BARD, CAMELOT, DISCUS, EQUINOX AND FLARE BOOKS

AVON BOOKS
A division of
The Hearst Corporation
959 Eighth Avenue
New York, New York 10019

Copyright © 1964 by Gregory McDonald.
Published by arrangement with the author.
Library of Congress Catalog Card Number: 64-16779
ISBN: 0-380-00924-2

First Avon Printing, February, 1977

AVON TRADEMARK REG. U.S. PAT. OFF. AND IN
OTHER COUNTRIES, MARCA REGISTRADA,
HECHO EN U.S.A.

Printed in the U.S.A.

To
Susi

PART I

The University

One

The University—ancient and venerable as it was—could be as squeamish as the management of a resort hotel about some things. Young people driven by compulsions beyond the comprehension of the academic mind were emitting anguished cries almost daily, in their rooms, in their parents' cars, in all the strange places they frequented. It was tragic; it was always tragic. But the act was usually committed by somebody's son, or a promising athlete the University had rescued from the Boston slums, or a fine young intellect-in-the-bud from Ohio or Illinois. This particular University, having produced three centuries of great men, was in the position of having to protect various images, of families, athletics and academics, by dealing with these situations quickly and quietly. There was never any fuss. The University, like any other producer, could not have its image publicly besmirched.

It was for this reason that on that late Sunday afternoon, when the telephone call came in to the basement office of the campus police, two officers proceeded unhurriedly to Mann Hall, crossing the sunlight-and-shade quadrangles without the least hope of finding anything unusual. One of them smoked.

They found the door to Suite 31 open a crack and, glancing at the two names on it, Betancourt and Case, pushed it open.

A boy of about nineteen was sitting in a chair facing the door, reading. There was no light in the room except for the twilight which came through the window. The room was decorated in the usual collegiate fashion, crimson and rich greens. It was difficult for the officers to see the boy's face, which was lowered and in shadow. He was obviously waiting for them, having left the door ajar; he looked, too, as if he might have been in the same chair, in much the same position, most of the afternoon. He looked up without lowering the book which he held in his hands, supported by his chest. On the table beside him was an empty bottle of soft drink.

"Case?"

The boy pointed toward the open bedroom door across the room. Then he said, almost as an afterthought, "I'm Betancourt."

The policemen went into the bedroom and found the other boy on one of the two beds, lying across it, face down. He was wearing a white shirt and dark slacks; part of his necktie stuck out from under him. His legs were drawn up in the position of someone climbing a mountain, and his hands were level with his head about eighteen inches away on either side. His hands clutched bunches of white sheet. The blood splattered all over the sheets came from his wrists which had been slashed.

The policemen did not touch him, but returned to the living room. Betancourt was still slumped in the chair, reading. One officer stopped to look at him, the other crossed the room to telephone for an ambulance. The boy really seemed to be reading; at least he did not look up from the book. He was wearing dark, neat slacks, polished loafers and white socks, a white shirt, red tie, and a light brown cashmere sweater. He was an extraordinarily handsome boy who had figured prominently on the University tennis team. He was always going back and forth across the yard, carrying two tennis racquets under his arm. There were several racquets in the room.

After telephoning, the first officer said, "He is Case, is he?"

He had a notebook and a pencil in his hands.

The boy said, "What?" His eyes continued to move back and forth across the page; the other officer continued to look at him.

"That boy in there is Case?"

"Yes," Betancourt said. He put the book face down on his chest and folded his hands over it. "McKensie Case."

"How old?"

"Nineteen."

"When did you find him?"

"I didn't find him. I watched him do it."

The policemen stared at him.

"What did you say?"

Betancourt reached out, took the empty bottle in his hands and stood it on the book.

"I said I saw him do it. I watched him. I didn't find him."

The first officer wrote nothing in his notebook. Betancourt glanced at him.

"I've been sitting here reading since about two o'clock. A half hour ago he came in and said he was going to do it. So he went into the bedroom and did it."

"And you didn't do anything about it?"

The boy was holding the bottle in front of his face, turning it around, as if concentrating on it. "No," he said. He tipped the top of the empty bottle toward him. "I went in and saw him," he said. "I stood in the

11

doorway and watched him. He was looking up at me from the sheet."

The policeman waited, still not writing anything. "Go on."

"Then he moved his head without raising it; he turned toward the wall, and he wasn't looking at me anymore."

"What did you do?"

"I came back and sat down and read a while. I finished the chapter, and then thought I had better call you."

The room was quiet and the policemen still. Betancourt went on playing with the bottle, turning it toward him and away from him, peering into the mouth of it each time.

"You mean you sat there and read while he went into the other room and killed himself."

Betancourt said, "Sure."

"Why?"

"He was free. He didn't call out for help. He didn't cry; you know what I mean?"

One of the policemen scratched his head under his hat, and the other lit a cigarette. The other officer was trying to meet Betancourt on his own terms, and this observation amused Betancourt. He noticed the frown on the policeman's face and smiled to himself. The second officer noticed this.

"Did you like this kid?"

"Sure. Liked him a lot."

"Known him long?"

"All through prep school. We were great friends. I'm sorry he's dead."

There was no emotion in the boy whatsoever. He might have been discussing the subject matter of the book he had been reading. His voice was low and controlled, his face expressionless. Despite what he was saying, he gave an impression of indifference, devoting his whole attention to the bottle in his hands. The first officer was writing something in his book and the second officer was studying him; but the boy did not ask or appear to wonder what they were writing or thinking.

The first officer said, "What did you say to him when he came in and said he was going to commit suicide?"

"Nothing."

The policeman looked up from the notebook on his knee. "Were you mad at him?"

"No."

"Did you hate him?"

"No."

"Did you want him dead?"

"No."

"Why didn't you stop him?" the other policeman asked.

"He was free."

The first policeman glanced at his partner, then went to the phone and made another call. Betancourt heard him ask for Doctor Wilson, the college psychiatrist. He heard him say, "A boy over here in Mann Hall just watched his roommate commit suicide, without doing anything to stop him. I think you had better come over. Suite thirty-one."

When he came away from the phone, the second officer, who was the younger, said to him. "Manslaughter?"

"I don't think so," said the first.

At that, the subject was dropped. However, the question had surprised Betancourt. He had not thought he might be guilty of manslaughter. He had done nothing but witness a rather messy and unfortunate act committed by someone else. He had had nothing to do with it. He held the bottle up to his eye, as if it were a telescope, and looked through it at the room.

"He was free."

The lights in the room were turned on when the ambulance men came, and Betancourt, from his chair, watched them carry the stretcher out of the bedroom, through the living room and out the door. He noticed they had difficulty getting it through the doors, as if they were carrying a cumbersome piece of furniture, but they did it smoothly all the same.

The proctor had come and stood at the door to the suite, leaning against the jamb. He was wearing a tweed jacket and was smoking a pipe. He said nothing, but moved out of the way when they brought the stretcher through. He left when Doctor Wilson arrived.

Doctor Wilson had seen the stretcher being carried down the stairwell. When he came into the suite, Betancourt stood up and shook hands. The doctor was about forty, wearing a heavy tweed suit and vest which fitted him perfectly. The boy noticed it was Harris tweed and custom made. The doctor was short, and, although a little heavy, looked athletic and powerful. He affected the short haircut favored by the students, although the style had come in well after his own college years. The policemen looked at Doctor Wilson and left without a word, closing the door.

Doctor Wilson sat down in the leather chair and lit a cigarette. Betancourt sat in the chair he had been in all afternoon, hanging his leg over one of the arms, to face Wilson.

Putting out the match with a shake of his hand, Wilson said, "Who's this fellow Case?"

"My roommate," Betancourt said. "My roommate which was."

"What's your first name?" Wilson asked the question

14

with a sharp look, as if he had just remembered something.

"Tom. Thomas Mathew."

"Tom Betancourt, the great New York lawyer. Is that your father?"

"Yes."

"Wasn't he President of the New York Bar at one time?"

"Yes."

Doctor Wilson took an ashtray off the table and put it in his lap, knocking his cigarette against the inside edge of it.

"Why did Case kill himself this afternoon?"

"I don't know."

"If you had killed yourself this afternoon, why would you have done it?"

Betancourt saw this question was designed to be shrewd. Why had he let Case kill himself this afternoon? He was not sure how to answer.

He was watching the psychiatrist knock the ash from his cigarette into the tray almost before there was any. He is not smoking, Tom thought to himself. He is simply feeding an ashtray.

The psychiatrist was waiting.

"No reason," said Tom. "I didn't kill myself."

"But you did let him kill himself."

"Yes."

"Why?"

"Why not? He was free. It's not as if it were an accident. He did it on purpose."

The cigarette tapping stopped and the psychiatrist looked directly at the boy. "Is that what you really believe?"

Tom looked down. "Yes. Why not?"

The psychiatrist sat there a moment longer, smoking. Then he said, "I don't know," and crushed out his cigarette.

He stood up and started towards the door; then, turned to look down at Tom.

"Was there anything between you two?"

"We were great friends," said Tom.

"I mean something more than that."

"Hell, no."

The psychiatrist looked at him a moment longer. "You're a handsome kid," he said.

"Thanks."

"Really handsome. You're almost a freak."

He took a pill from a case he carried in his pocket and put it on the table.

"That's a sedative," he said. "Take it if you need it."

"Will I need it?"

"You might."

There was a knock on the door, and Wilson opened it. The proctor was standing there, not coming in.

He said to Doctor Wilson, "The Dean called. Betancourt is to be at a Dean's Conference Tuesday afternoon at three, at Grant Hall."

"All right," Wilson said. He looked around at Tom to make sure he had heard.

"That is unusual, isn't it?" the proctor said. He peered through the door at Tom.

Tom knew the psychiatrist was about to leave. Tom had risen when Doctor Wilson had entered the room. Now, on his departure, he was not offering the man a similar courtesy. The man had accomplished nothing.

Doctor Wilson said, "You call me if you need me. If something goes wrong, or if you just want to talk, you call me up or come over to the house. Do you understand?"

Tom said, "Yes."

After they had gone, he remained in his chair. He looked at the book on the table, and the bottle, and the ash tray with the ashes from Doctor Wilson's cigarette in it. For a moment he swung his foot in a pendulum motion. His hand was on the arm of his chair under his knee. He looked about the room, picking out the things which belonged to him, and the things which belonged to Case. The four cameras on the mantelpiece and the one on the desk were his own. The sweater and the jacket on the divan belonged to Case. All the tennis racquets belonged to him, but the pair of sneakers under the leather chair belonged to Case. Roughly half the books belonged to Case. They would have to be gone through. He could not remember to whom the desk set belonged. It had been given to one of them for Christmas two years before.

He went and stood at the window, looking down at the quadrangle. He could see the lamp posts and the circles of light under them, and he ran his eyes along the sidewalks which went around the quadrangle coming in and out of the circles of light. The snow had been gone for a long time, and the grass was of uniform darkness. There were no patches of mud and dirt anymore. He had seen the patches dug up and planted some time before, and now there was green grass there.

He turned to the desk and picked up the phone, asking the operator for a Lehigh number in New York. Mary answered, and Tom asked for his mother.

She came to the phone and started by saying, "I'm eating. Don't you ever eat, Tom?"

"Do you know where Dad is?" he asked.

"Why? What's the matter?"

He waited, but she did not go on.

"Where is Dad?"

17

"He's in Washington, I think, Sweetie. Are you in trouble?"

"Will you find out where he is and have him call me?"

"All right. But you're not in trouble, are you?"

"Just have him call me."

He hung up and threw himself on the divan, looking at the ceiling. He reached over and turned on the hi-fidelity, and then lay there listening to the music. It played *The 1812 Overture* and then a recording of Dixieland made by Turk Murphy. He went to the small refrigerator and took out a bottle of soft drink, bringing it back with him and tipping it down his throat without sitting up. The phonograph played Frank Sinatra singing love songs.

The telephone rang and he clicked off the hi-fi to answer it.

His father's voice said, "Tom, your mother said you wanted me to call you."

"Yes," he said.

"What's the matter?"

"Casey killed himself this afternoon."

His father said, quietly, "I'm sorry, Tom."

"I just wanted you to know I may be leaving the University soon."

"Is that necessary?"

"I may be expelled. There is going to be a meeting Tuesday afternoon and they may expel me."

"Why you? What did you have to do with it?"

"Casey killed himself in my presence. I watched him."

"How did he do it?"

"He cut his wrists."

His father said nothing, for a short moment.

"Do they have you in any sort of legal custody?" he asked.

"No. They mentioned manslaughter because I watched him die."

"That's nonsense. They can't hold you for that. Look," he continued, "I'm leaving for Venezuela tonight but I'll be back by the end of the week. The University won't do anything before then. Universities move very slowly. I'll come up to Boston when I get back."

"All right."

"I'm going down to see Mister Francini. Do you remember Mister Francini?"

"No."

"He was out at Sparrow's Point with us last summer. He has a very beautiful daughter."

"Everybody has a very beautiful daughter."

His father said, "I'm sorry about Casey. Why don't you go out and buy yourself a beer."

"I can't. I'm in Massachusetts and they don't sell beer to minors."

"I forgot. Don't run afoul of the law. I'll see you at the end of the week."

The conversation was over, and Tom went back to the hi-fi, turning it on. He had carefully taken the needle off the recording when the phone began to ring, and now he put it back, at the beginning of the record.

He then went into the bathroom and brushed his teeth. He hated the sweetness of soft drinks.

Two

Tom Betancourt was a camera fan. It was a hobby he had picked up when he was about nine years old. Someone in the family had given him a camera for Christmas, and he took to it the way young boys will, going around snapping pictures of everybody and everything for the remainder of the holidays, some days using up as much as six rolls of film. These first pictures were just what anyone would expect. He still had prints of a few of them, somewhere. There was one snapshot of his cocker spaniel sitting in front of a white door with his red Christmas ribbon around his neck. He looked very perky. There was another of his mother, surrounded by a group of her friends, toasting the New Year. He had taken that from the stairs of the New York town house. She looked flushed and filled with enthusiasm over the prospect of the inevitable new year.

Gradually, however, he learned the first lesson of the young artist. He learned not to be careless with the mechanical instrument of his art. He began taking pictures with great caution, not arranging the subject as he wanted it, but waiting for it to go through a fairly predictable motion until it reached the one pose that typified it. In this way, he learned to watch and wait, catching the essence of his subject quickly. He began doing his own developing. He turned a large closet which was a part of his room in the house on East 70th Street into a dark room, using the smaller closet for his suits and shoes. He arranged to have a running-water system set up, connecting with the plumbing of his bath, so he could have a basin, which was essential to the process, in the dark room. He arranged shelves with the various bottles of the chemicals necessary, and had stacks of paper at hand. It was a rule among the family, and the first lesson the servants learned, that when Tom was in the "dark room," no one was to try to get in or ask him to come out. No servant was ever allowed to clean in there.

His camera became more professional, a large part of his year's allowance being spent in the specialty shops in New York. He would spend almost his whole vacations from school in these shops, asking about this and that. The shopkeepers were always glad to see him, because he had the money to spend on the equipment he wanted. Besides that, he knew cameras.

His photographs became more and more remarkable. He would spend hours prowling the woods around the family's Long Island country home, at Sparrow's Point, in any sort of weather. He went through a period, when he was twelve and thirteen, when he would construct complicated trip mechanisms in the woods, so that an animal would inadvertently take a picture of itself. He lost a good camera this way once, leaving it out during a night when it unexpectedly snowed. As he grew older, he would walk around cities for whole days and nights at a time, his camera with him, watching the people and taking an occasional picture. He developed a system, using two cameras and an attaché case, which allowed him to take pictures without the subject's knowing it. Besides that, he always had a large camera hanging from a strap around his neck. Some of his photographs were remarkably artistic. There was a picture of a fat blind man in a top hat sitting on a door-stoop in the slums, playing an accordian and singing to some children. The children were swarming all over him. The man's rough face and clothes surrounded by the pink and tender-looking children against the red, chipping brick of the building and the rubbish on the gray sidewalk made quite a study. Tom never missed a riot, if one should be within reach. He was always there, passing in and out among the crowd with his attaché case. Although he did not care for spectator sports, he frequently went to football and wrestling matches, almost completely ignoring the contest. He would be looking at the people, studying them while their attention was on the sport; once or twice he would find a surprisingly good picture in his camera when he returned home. He once had an action photo in a weekly picture magazine, winning a prize for it. His father had arranged with the editors to have it printed in the magazine, but this had happened only once. As is always the case with the sons of moderately successful men, the presumption was that Tom would choose a career in law.

The camera was second nature to him. He never went out, even to a class, without it. He knew interesting things could happen in the dullest of places, and people were frequently surprised to discover, after the excitement of some unexpected event had subsided, that Tom had a perfect record of it. His pictures were regularly shown in the college newspaper. Another reason he always wore the camera was so that people would get used to seeing him with it. They were always self-conscious at first, he noticed, when they saw a camera. It was instinctive for them to keep smiling and posing until the camera was used and they knew there was no more film. Therefore, he never appeared without a camera, even if he should be without film, so that people would lose their self-consciousness around him. Tom Betancourt, being a good artist, built up trust in his society so he could live in it and still practice his art. He seldom took a picture, but when he did so it was the result of a great deal of observation and thought and was always clearly expressive. He practiced his art assiduously.

Therefore the people who saw him walking through the college square that night were not surprised to see him carrying a camera, in spite of what had happened that afternoon. They all knew about it, of course, or most of them did. The University kept these situations out of the newspaper, but still, within the University itself, news traveled fast. Both Tom Betancourt and McKensie Case had been popular and well-known around the University. Besides having his pictures produced almost daily in the newspaper, Tom was one of the principal members of the college tennis team. The defeat of Princeton the season before was largely accredited to him. Case had been known for his jazz trumpet playing, and besides that was thought of as a generally amiable, easygoing sort of person. He was the type you would like to have date your sister. People were always setting him up for football weekends and only once did he complicate matters by falling in love with his date. She fell in love with him, too, but they both had to finish school, so she returned to Vassar to write letters. The letters stopped after a while, and the whole matter, after a few weeks, was forgotten. Of the two boys, Casey was the more personable and probably the better liked, but they were both admired. Tom was regarded as highly as Casey, but in a different way. Many people at the University had already accepted Tom's hard shell. He knew these people would not be too surprised to see him walking around after Casey's death as if nothing had happened.

Tom had left his rooms about seven-thirty, thinking he would walk to the Square for a hamburger. The house dining room closed at seven-fifteen, but Tom would have avoided it anyway. He knew the people who normally flocked to his table would not come, but would glance at him from across the hall as if he had changed suddenly and without warning. He knew his presence would embarrass others, and would stimulate conversations no one would find comfortable. People would feel obliged to say the proper things to each other about Casey's death. They would express wonder, as they talked quietly to each other, about Tom's role in the affair. Tom had always hated being the subject of conversation.

When he reached the Square and saw the theatre marquee, he remembered it was Sunday and there would be a new film showing. Usually by Sunday night he had studied enough to warrant going to a movie. He had gradually developed the habit of seeing what was playing each Sunday night. People with whom he had eaten supper at Mann Hall usually went along with him, even if only a Western were playing. There was seldom anything else to do Sunday nights. He looked at his watch and saw he was in plenty of time; the only thing he would miss would be the news. He did not care much what was playing, nor did he care about the hamburger. Tom could start out for a hamburger and not care if he did not get it for three hours. He was seldom aware of being hungry.

He bought a candy bar inside the theatre, and slumped into his seat to watch the film, undoing the wrapper, but not tasting the candy until it began to melt in his hand. He had purposely chosen a seat with several empty seats on either side of him. He always did that. He had developed these habits and practiced them religiously. He never sat next to anyone on a bus,

24

and was always slightly annoyed if someone sat next to him. In the dining hall he never joined other students, but always looked for an empty table. It was a large hall and, as he always ate late, there was usually a good chance of finding one. Invariably, however, others would come over to his table, and within minutes it would be filled up and extra chairs would have to be brought. People would join them without encouragement. Tom never knew why, but he had guessed it was simply because he was a physically attractive person and could always be trusted to regard everyone with utmost courtesy. He never committed the sin of intruding into anyone else's life, but his aloofness subtly communicated the warning that no one was to intrude too far into his life either. He only allowed people to approach him on his own terms.

He felt this same tinge of annoyance coming out of the theatre, when he saw Mavis Oliver approaching him. He could not tell whether she had been in the theatre or waiting for him outside. The theatre was just closing for the night and people were swarming out from the last show.

Mavis had dated Case, but apparently without any strong feeling for him. Case had been more attracted to her than she to him. She had sometimes refused to go out with him. She would always go if Betancourt was going too, even though he was dating someone else. It had been obvious, and amusing, to both the boys that she went out with Case purely to see Betancourt. Case had quickly discovered the infallible way of getting Mavis to go out with him was to get Betancourt to go out, too. As soon as she heard it was to be a double date with Tom, she would accept, without hesitation, Case's invitation. Tom felt slightly perturbed at seeing Mavis, wondering what she wanted; but he always did, at seeing anybody. He was bound to be polite.

She stepped up to him, crossing the lines of people coming out of the theatre.

They were under the light of the marquee; the Square around them was dark.

"I knew you would be here," she said. "The great Tom Betancourt wouldn't miss his Sunday night movie even if his best friend did just bleed to death all over the floor."

"He didn't bleed to death all over the floor."

"Where did he bleed to death?" Mavis said.

"All over the bed."

Her eyes were slits, as she looked up at him.

"You're a son-of-a-bitch," she said.

The last of the people were coming out of the theatre, stepping around them. They were all looking at the boy and the girl. Mavis was leaning towards Betancourt on her toes, her head up and her fists clenched. Only good manners kept the people moving.

"What are you doing here, Mavis? Going to see a movie the night your old beau died."

"I came here because I knew you would be here. I came to call you a murderer."

Betancourt looked away from the girl's eyes. There was pure hatred in them.

"I'm sorry," he said. "I'm sorry I said that about your coming to the movies. I didn't believe you were serious."

"You're incredible."

"I just forget about emotions," he said. "He died because he wanted to."

She looked at him meaningfully. "I hope you want to die, too."

Tom looked at her, mildly stunned. He was not going to argue with her; her emotions were no concern of his. He was too surprised to argue anyway.

More composed, she stood away from him. "What the hell makes you tick, Tom Betancourt?"

He took the question seriously. "I don't know."

"You even have your camera around your neck." She made a gesture of impatience at it. "Tell me, did you take a picture of Casey while he was dying?"

He looked down at the camera. "No."

"That's a wonder. It's really a wonder you didn't pop flashlights in his face as he was passing out."

"Flash bulbs."

Her eyes slits, she made a curious animal noise, one of sheer exasperation. She threw her arms around herself, hitting her shoulders with both fists. Her eyes clouded then, and Tom thought he was seeing them through thick glass. She was crying.

"Do you want a hamburger?" he asked.

She turned from him abruptly and walked away, head down. Tom stood under the marquee watching her for some time. The lights of the marquee over his head went off.

Several thoughts went through his head. He wondered if she had been in love with Casey after all, or if she had simply resented the friendship of the two boys in some strange, feminine way. Tom supposed that to Mavis he would appear the stronger of the two. But why should Mavis care about him? He had never expressed any interest in her, or encouraged her even slightly. He had never thought about her enough even to reject her. She had been introduced to him as Casey's date, and he had never thought of her otherwise. This was not out of a collegiate sense of honor. It had not occurred to him to covet his roommate's date, or to not covet her. He had simply had no interest in her. He could not see any reason for the intensity of her emotion.

He turned away then, and walked a short way down

27

the street to a drugstore. He looked in the window and saw it was not too crowded. There were a few city workers at the counter, and one or two students. Tom saw where he could sit. There was a stool empty, with empty stools on each side of it. He was reaching for the door handle when he heard Mavis scream.

He paused in the light from the drugstore window.

She was across the dark square, and he could not have seen her even if he had looked. But he heard her scream at the top of her lungs, and each word was clear and slow and separated from the last.

"Tom Betancourt! I hate your guts!"

Tom halted only a moment at the door to the drug-store, and then opening it, went in and took his seat at the counter.

Eating his hamburger in relative peace, he presumed the Case family would feel inexplicable bitterness toward him, too. He thought their son's death, despite everything, would be an awful shock to them. He supposed the Cases, in keeping with modern custom, had encouraged independence and resourcefulness in their children. But what a shock it would be for them to realize how one child had elected to express his freedom. He had been free enough to kill himself. But Tom thought of it coldly and analytically. He was not sure whether he would offer them any sympathy.

For a moment, he thought he should get on a train and attend the funeral. After all, he and Casey had gone through preparatory school together, always as roommates and best friends. They had shared each other's interests and worries. They had studied together and fretted over the same subjects. They had talked to each other about sex, one calming the other down with misinformation, the second creating anxieties in the other with misinformation. They told each other about their first forays into sexual experience as they happened, crowing with complete impunity. It had been a happy moment in both their lives when they succeeded in getting into the same University. They had been pleased at the thought of being able to room together for another four years. They had been more than best friends; they had enjoyed a relationship all too infrequent between brothers. Like an old married couple, they had become completely used to each other, and took each other for granted. Despite all this, Betancourt knew the Case family would not want him at Casey's funeral. They had undoubtedly been told by the authorities, gently enough, but factually, of the role Tom had played in Casey's death. Their reaction to the news would be purely emotional. His being at the funeral would make them uncomfortable, if not enraged.

Missing the funeral did not bother him too much; such things were against his instincts anyway.

Three

The next day, Monday, Tom did not even think of
going to class. The prospect of facing his classmates did
not bother him too much for his own sake. Rather, he
realized his presence would embarrass people and
make them uncomfortable. He had felt the same way
the night before, when thinking of going to the dining
hall, and it was his habit to place the greatest possible
distance between himself and other people's emotions.

Instead, he spent the day packing Casey's trunks.
The first thing he had done upon arising was to rip the
sheets off Casey's bed and burn them. He had wanted
to do this the night before, but the blood had not been
dry. Then he emptied the closets, bureau and book-
shelves, bringing all of Casey's things into the living
room. It was ten o'clock before he was able to go
downstairs to get the trunk and twenty minutes past ten
before he and the houseman had hauled it up to the
third floor.

Doing these things was his job. It was understood, in
tragic circumstances, that the packing up was left to the
roommate. It was an unwritten law. It was never to be
left to the family, for they seldom came to the school
again, especially in the case of suicide. It would have
been embarrassing for the University and the students
to have them come. It was Tom's job therefore, and he

did it as well as he could, and without feeling. It did not matter to him if the rest of the world, including the dead boy's family, believed him responsible for the death. Nor did care about not going to the funeral. The trunk had to be packed. It was his job to pack it.

The suits and socks, shoes and shirts were an easy matter. He knew without hesitation which belonged to Case. They had borrowed back and forth endlessly, one fitting the other out with a tie or shirt as needed, but there was never any doubt in their minds as to what belonged to whom. The records and books were a different matter. Frequently, taking a course together, they would save money by buying one book, going halves on it. Then each would have books of his own, which the other would read. Records were usually bought with the consent of both; the purchaser was the one who had extra money that week. They had similar tastes in these matters, and it was hard separating the results. If there was any doubt in his mind, over a given object, such as the desk set, he put it in the trunk. He did not want it. He was exact in this as he was in all other things, although the waste struck him as impractical. He knew these goods would do the Case family no good, except as sentimental mementoes to put in their son's room, whereas he himself would most certainly have future use for them. The thought came to him more than once, too, that the Cases had no idea what things Casey had owned. They would recognize none of these things.

Emptying Casey's desk, Tom found a picture in a drawer and looked at it closely. He had seen it before. Casey had told him it was of his sister, Ellen. It was not a good picture, but it showed an attractive girl looking into a camera, smiling, seeming not to care that her blond hair was in disorder. The impression she

31

created in the picture was the same Casey had created in life. He was obviously the well-loved son of a warm, happy family. She appeared to be just as sure of herself.

Now Tom had to ask himself just how warm and happy the Case family could have been. Close as he had been to Casey, he had never met his sister. He had never met any of his family. This fact had never struck Tom as being significant before. Now, sitting cross-legged on the floor, looking at the picture of Ellen Case, he paused to wonder about it.

None of the Cases had ever come to either the preparatory school or the University. They had never dropped in at the Betancourts' town house on East 70th Street, although Tom knew they had been through New York many times. After all, it was the usual thing to do, to stop in at the house of your son's best friend. They had never shown any interest in meeting him or his parents.

He remembered that on the day he and Casey were graduating from prep school, the Case family was in New York boarding a ship bound for Southampton. Casey had come home with Tom and spent most of that summer with him at Sparrow's Point. In fact, thinking of it, Tom realized that although Casey had spent most of his holidays with Tom, either in New York during the winter, or at Sparrow's Point in the summer, Tom had never spent any time with the Case family. He had never even seen them.

He knew they existed because there was an occasional letter, and someone always called from home on Christmas Eve and on Casey's birthday. It was a routine, one communication Casey was sure of receiving, and the call always came on time. However, he had seldom spoken of his family; although, when pressed by polite inquiry at table, he had given facts of their existence.

His father was an architect, and they lived in New Hope, Pennsylvania. They also had a winter place in West Palm Beach, Florida, and a summer place in Yarmouth, Massachusetts. Ellen, one year younger than he, was usually at some school or other. Beyond these matters he never went. He was able to recite these few facts of his family as if he had once seen a dossier on them. Tom had stopped being curious about them a long time before, assuming then that Casey was not at all reluctant to speak of his family but just did not know that much about them. They were forever traveling from one home to another and Casey was always allowed to explain their absence (such as at Commencement) by simply saying they were not there. At Christmas time, when he was in Massachusetts, they were in Florida. In the summer, when he would be leaving Massachusetts for a camp in North Carolina, they would just be coming up to their Yarmouth house. Tom knew that Casey saw his family, but only at infrequent intervals, and never for long. When they did send for him, Casey would be put on a plane or train by the Betancourt household. But Tom had never been invited to go home with him. This relationship had never struck him as particularly unusual until he found the photograph of Ellen.

Although he could not go to the funeral, he wanted to know the Case family. He was especially curious about Ellen. He asked himself how close she could be to her family. He was teased by the desire to meet her. The photograph of Ellen was the only possession of Casey's he did not pack. Tom put it with his own things.

Some of the belongings were undoubtedly Casey's. The two trumpets, for example, Tom wrapped in

33

sheets, despite their leather covers. The several mouth-pieces he put in the shoes. The sheets of music went in with the books, including the few pieces Casey had written himself. Tom wondered if anyone else would ever play them.

He also recognized, with a surprising clarity, things belonging to Casey as gifts he had once given him. For Christmas when they were both about fourteen, Tom had given Casey a pair of solid, white gold cuff links, with trumpets etched on them. He held them in his hand now, wondering what had ever possessed him to spend so much money on a gift for anybody. He must have been mad. He also found the Zippo lighter he had given Casey last birthday, and threw that in the trunk as well. When he was all through, he sat on the floor by the open trunk, continuing to wonder about the gold cuff links. Had he been showing off in making such a gift?—or had he gone to this expense to express some-thing real that had existed between them?—The not knowing, the being unable to pin this relationship down to precise mathematical formulae bothered him. He had to know about these things. He had to lay words here and actions there on the floor in front of him, right out where he could see them and cooly calculate their individual importance. He was not sentimental, but he wondered if he ever had been. He wanted to know, as matter-of-factly as another person might ask about his train schedule, exactly what emotions or feel-ings had ever been involved. It was beyond him. He could not remember. He had lived with McKensie Case for almost as long as he could remember, being used to him and taking him for granted. He surmised that there had probably been great love between them, but he did not know. There had never been sexual tension that he was aware of, nor had there ever been any sexual expression. And yet there were the cuff links which mutely indicated to him that there had been a feeling of love, which had consciously expressed itself at least this once. If there had been such a feeling, it was beyond him now.

He left the lid of the trunk open, knowing he would be sure to find things he had missed. Looking at his watch, he was surprised to find it was five o'clock. More out of necessity than anything else, he put on his jacket and went out to eat a hamburger.

He did not close the trunk until the next morning, Tuesday, when he made tags for it and the other suitcases, addressing them,

McKensie Case, Esq.
New Hope
Penna.

He was not sure what return address to put on the tags, but finally wrote in the name and address of the University, although he realized it was probably futile to do so. Whoever took care of those things for the University would have no idea what to do with the luggage, if it ever came back. He then latched the trunk, affixing the tags to the aluminum handles, piling the suitcases on top of it. They made quite a pile, in the middle of the living room, and he stood back and looked at it. He went to the desk and picked up his camera and walked around the pile, studying it. He leaned a tennis racquet against the pile, slightly at an angle, and took a picture of it. It struck him as a typically collegiate scene.

He spent most of Tuesday morning out on the river, rowing. He seldom used a shell; he only rowed for exercise, never with the crew. He preferred the wherry. It was a much more stable boat, and besides, he believed it gave him greater exercise. He had never gone

35

out for any team sports, winning all his letters in tennis. He was undoubtedly one of the school's best singles tennis players, with a fast, clean serve and an almost ruthless return. Unlike most of his collegiate competitors it was impossible to rattle him. The tension of the game just did not seem to build up in him, and he always had the edge over his competitors on the game point. The fact that this serve, return, or rally would decide the match never fazed him; he therefore had the upper hand and usually won. But it was a game one played individually, facing one's competitor, not like crew where one was obliged to act as a member of a team. The thought of team work always annoyed him, and after a few early experiences, he would not consider joining a team. He discovered that when they were all happy and excited they worked together beautifully, but when one was disgruntled for some reason or another, it spoiled the whole show. He ruled emotion quite out of his own work. He played tennis as he had learned and practiced it; he never played because he was happy or wanted to beat somebody. He rowed in the same way: sweep, stroke, sweep, stroke, cracking his wrists precisely, sending the feathers into the water without causing a ripple, watching his knees come up together, the muscles in his legs working smoothly and simultaneously. It did not matter if he was out on the river all by himself while the rest of the students were at class. The people going along the Embankment Highway in cars would not know good rowing from bad rowing, and if they did, they would not have the time or the interest to notice. He went two miles straight up the river without even looking up at the bridges as he went under them, or breaking his rhythm, or going very far from exact midstream. When he stopped he laid the oar feathers flat on the water and held them steady with his elbows while he examined a blister on his left hand. Sweat was coming down from his hair and getting in his eyes, but it did not bother him; he blinked his eyes clear. Then he rowed back to the boathouse in much the same manner and at the same pace, leaving it for the dock man to put up the boat. He walked to his rooms, showered and dressed in his blue suit and walked over to Grant Hall for the Dean's Conference. It was exactly three o'clock when he arrived, although he had not looked at his watch in an hour and a half.

The conference was held in a room reserved by the Administration solely for this sort of situation. Tom knew the room had been a campus conversation piece. It was at the top of an old building, with Gothic beamed ceilings. The room had been decorated originally some centuries ago with great ugly oil portraits of unknown alumni along the walls. Within recent history, someone in the Administration had ordered the room done over, and, in keeping with the general idea of modernization, the paintings were removed and the walls painted a pastel green. It was only a matter of weeks before someone realized that certain trusts and bequests in favor of the University were dependent upon those paintings being left on the walls. The University was not one to violate a trust, so the paintings went back up, the somber old alumni in their Puritan garb and Puritan faces looking odd surrounded by pastel green. The Administration thought this a good room to meet the students in. It was good for little else.

Assembled now were the proctor from Mann Hall, whom Betancourt had passed many times but had never spoken to, the Dean who was in charge of whatever category Betancourt was in (he had spoken to him

37

once, the year before, at a get-together dinner) and the college psychiatrist, Doctor Wilson. None of them stood up when Betancourt entered, and the Dean did not look up. He had papers on the desk before him. It was the Doctor who suggested Tom sit down.

Tom remained standing. Without any preface, he said, "I want you to know before you say anything that I hope to leave the University as soon as possible. I have advised my father to that effect and I have a letter stating that intention, addressed to the Dean, in my pocket."

The Dean looked up then, measuring Tom with his eyes. There had been nothing disrespectful or sullen in the boy's tone of voice. Neither had there been anything particularly respectful. It had been a flat speech, delivered with the utmost efficiency.

The Dean asked, blankly, "Why, before we say anything?"

Tom said quietly, "Save you the bother."

"Are you afraid of what we might say, Tom?" Doctor Wilson's voice was soft and slow.

Tom said, "No."

Looking at him, they could not doubt him. There was no sign of fear in him.

"I don't think I care what you say," Tom said. "I honestly think I do not care what you would have to say." He stopped and looked at the three men. Then Tom looked down. "I do not mean any discourtesy."

The men, sitting at the table, waited.

Tom raised his eyes to them again.

"I want to know one thing," he said. "Is there a charge of manslaughter being brought against me?"

"No," the Dean said easily. "We've been in contact with the District Attorney and there is no criminal complaint being brought against you at all. I'm afraid

38

your complicity in the crime is rather moral than legal."

The Dean waited to see if this comment would cause a reaction from Tom. There was none.

"Tell me, Tom. Why do you want to leave?"

The Dean was regarding him with an almost clinical interest.

Tom glanced at the psychiatrist. He had already thought what a dreadful intrusion he could expect in his life if he were to remain at the University.

"I would no longer feel free here," he said.

"Were you afraid we might expel you?" the Dean asked.

"I had thought of it."

The Dean spoke to his hands, folded on the table. "It is not the policy of the University to expel people because they have done something we do not understand. We frankly do not understand what you have done. It would normally be our goal to pursue this matter further, with psychiatric counsel, and any other means at our disposal. In putting yourself out of our reach, you may be putting yourself out of reach of help."

Tom said, "I understand."

He took the letter from his pocket and laid it on the table with the other papers that were there, all concerning himself. It was a simple, efficient act, totally lacking in drama.

He then looked at the Dean. Tom was clearly waiting to have this meeting come to an end, although there was no impatience in his manner.

"Tell me, Betancourt," the Dean said. "Are you entirely a product of private education?"

"Yes, sir. Completely."

The Dean sighed, glancing down the length of the

table. Then he looked up at Tom and said something Tom thought rather surprising.

"God bless you, Tom."

"Thank you, sir."

Four

By Thursday morning he was packed and ready to go. He had phoned his mother in New York and asked to have the car sent up. John arrived in the big Mercedes before noon. Tom was waiting for him at the gate, sitting on his luggage. It was a nice spring day, although still a little cool. He enjoyed the feeling of sun through his clothes. It was a surprisingly warm sun.

He saw the Mercedes coming down the Embankment Highway and stood up. John stuck his head out the window and waved before crossing the oncoming traffic and coming into the little driveway to the iron-grilled, closed gate.

He jumped out of the car and they shook hands. John was a large Swiss, with massive hands and an enormous mouth completely filled with very white teeth. He looked well in his black uniform.

"How are you, John? How's Mary?"

"She's okay. She's fine. How about yourself?"

John, who served as butler-chauffeur, had married Mary, the house-maid, soon after he came to work for the Betancourts after the war. The two formed the permanent staff, doing their work in the way only Swiss can. Nothing was ever out of place in the house; there was never a dirty ashtray, or a wastebasket with even an old letter in it. The car was kept sparkling. Everything was always immaculate. The cook was a different question entirely. She was the cloud on everybody's horizon. Mrs. Betancourt could never keep a cook. There was a constant turnover, of new Mamies and Hannahs, every few months. It had got so Tom never went into the kitchen when he was home for a holiday. It was not worth making the acquaintance of whomever might be there. She would not be there the next time he was home. Tom thought all cooks must be idealists. They are always sure there is a better kitchen in the next house, although the kitchen Mrs. Betancourt had arranged for them could not have been better. It created a situation in the staff, because John and Mary always had to back down and let the cook have her way, although they had been with the family longer and knew better how things should be done. They never seemed to mind, however, always being willing to back down with grace and a grin.

Tom respected them enormously. He thought it might be because they were Swiss that they were so self-disciplined, both to their jobs and to their sense of personal duty. He had heard that about the Swiss. John and Mary were always in the background somewhere, like his mother's pictures on the wall, functional and at the same time charming. He was always aware of John and Mary, and he knew the respect and liking he had for them was mutual. He supposed they liked him because they saw and respected his self-discipline. Many times, when he was growing up, he knew that John and Mary had understood why he had absented himself from the company of the family—purposely to avoid a crisis or an unpleasant scene. They knew Tom to be extraordinarily considerate. Sometimes Tom's presence would not be wanted at dinner and Mary would bring a tray to him in his room. Nothing would ever be said. They were simply working together to make things run smoothly.

While he and John were packing the trunk of the car, Tom saw a friend come through one of the doors of the quadrangle, stopping to look across at him. They had eaten together, played tennis together and attended class together. Once, the two of them, with three others, had spent a skiing weekend in Quebec. The boy stood for a few moments, watching from across the courtyard. It must have been obvious to him what Tom was doing at the car. But the boy did not come over or wave. Instead, he turned around and went back through the door. Tom could hear the hinges squeak as the door closed.

Then, when Tom was lifting a heavy case into the trunk, John said, "Where is your friend, Casey? He is always here."

Tom guessed John had heard nothing about what had happened. That surprised him, because there was little the servants did not know. Passing from one room to another, putting scraps of paper away, hearing halves of telephone conversations, they usually knew about everything. Tom wondered if everyone had been too horrified by Casey's death to speak of it. Even then, he thought, the servants would be able to guess something from the silence. Of course, there was no reason why John should not know about it. John was one of his best friends; he had always called the son of the house, "Tom," and was not above roughing him up playfully and calling him obscene names with affection. Tom, on the other hand, as a joke that had started some years ago, called the servant, John, "Sir." Death duties ruled out the possibility of John's ever becoming Tom's own servant, and they both knew it. This allowed a wonderful familiarity. John never went beyond his bounds, though. Doing so would have made Tom uncomfortable and John knew it. It was an ideal relationship.

Tom decided to answer the question simply.

"Casey is dead," he said.

Although his back was turned to John, Tom, having his head in the trunk of the car, could feel how startled John was. Standing up, he glanced at John and saw surprise and hurt in John's face. Tom had not realized it but John had probably had as much liking for Casey as he had for Tom himself. Casey had been one of the family for as long as John had been with them. Tom was pleased by John's reaction. He was glad the servant felt real sorrow. But there would be no more questions from John, and Tom appreciated that.

The trunk was closed and they were ready to go.

Tom said. "May I drive, Sir?"

John smiled. "You think you are a safe driver?"

There was another old joke between them. John had taught the boy to drive in the grounds of the place at Sparrow's Point.

"I don't know," said Tom, taking the keys John held out to him. "Got any insurance?"

They turned out of the driveway and into the Embankment Highway. Tom was a good driver. He guided the big car through the city traffic smoothly and quickly. John had taught him the knack of studying the behavior of the other drivers on the road as one came up to them so that one could think one's way around them without varying one's pace a single mile-per-hour. If the speed limit were fifty, John drove at exactly fifty, never at forty-nine or fifty-one. When he came up to cars going slower, he studied them and did whatever was necessary to get around or through them. Other cars never got in his way. Tom had learned this trick from him. They had a common spirit in this regard. Driving was not a job or a fight or a challenge. It was something one did as a sport or a musical exercise, flawlessly and with discipline. It was a splendid technique. Given any driving job, either one of them could get from here to there in less time than anybody else, and yet neither of them ever broke the speed limit. At Auburndale they turned from Route 128 into the Massachusetts Highway, stopping at the Toll Gate. There was little traffic on the highway.

John, sitting in the seat beside Tom, said, "You are coming home early this year, aren't you?"

John was always confused as to how things worked in this country, such as school terms. All he knew was that he was picking Tom up in early April rather than in early June. He would have believed anything.

"Yes," Tom said. "I'm not finishing the year out."

John looked at him apprehensively. "Will you be able to go back to the University?"

"Yes, of course. I'm leaving because I want to."

He knew John would guess from that answer that his leaving was in some way related to Casey's death. He was amused to think that John, being gentle and tenderhearted, was doubtlessly crediting Tom with great feeling over the death of his friend. He was happy to leave it at that. He did not mind John's thinking their feelings were similar.

The driving was fairly easy. They were going by New Haven almost before they knew it. Outside New Haven they stopped at a place for sandwiches and coffee, sitting at a counter together. John always felt a little conspicious in his uniform out of New York, although on the whole he liked the uniform very much. Both realized that the other people in the lunch room, the truck drivers and waitresses, were gaping at them. People were apt to gape at Tom anyway; but when he was with a uniformed chauffer, his personal attractiveness seemed to be even more enhanced.

John drove the rest of the way, guiding the car effortlessly and artfully. He always had the thought that everyone on the road was watching him, recognizing him as a great driver. It was true that every time he went out on the highway, another car was sure to follow him for miles, doing the exact things John was doing to get through the traffic. Tom sat slumped in the seat next to him, watching the monotonous gray Connecticut countryside going by, sprinkled as it was, with cheap, post-war houses. He hated the thought of those houses, which had been thrown up quickly and carelessly, and sold for much more than they were worth. They were only shacks and would not last long. Looking at them made him worry about his fellow countrymen. Since the War, almost everyone had come to accept carelessness and cheap construction as a matter of course. There was no such thing as quality material. He closed his eyes against them. He would not let himself see the indication of softness on the part of his fellow citizens.

Riding along in the smooth car, his eyes closed, Tom Betancourt began to experience a new sensation. First, he felt a little dizzy; he had the impression the world, as a mass, was pulling away from him, to the left. He had to tighten his muscles to bring it back into focus. The effort made him feel nauseous; more than once he was about to call out to John to stop the car, afraid he was about to vomit. He kept his mouth clamped tightly closed and breathed deeply. He had learned a long time ago he could overcome these expressions of emotion by breathing with control. He had learned, when a little boy, that by controlling his breath he could even resist crying. It seemed to help in this instance. His body became more relaxed, although he still felt his stomach to be upset and kept his jaw shut tight. He supposed this was happening because he had not been eating carefully the last few days.

Then, images began to come clearly to his mind. He

had never been imaginative and had never allowed himself a day dream in his life. Being taken up with photography, he only saw what was in front of him, with a disciplined, trained eye. He would never visualize what was not there. He could not create faces of people who were not in front of him. Nor could he remember what people had said, or what they might say in a projected circumstance. He never projected circumstances. However, this once, just as they were turning onto the Merritt Parkway, images of people's faces, complete with expressions, came welling up toward him. It was completely involuntary . He could not stop them. First, he saw his old dog, the cocker spaniel, and then his mother as she held out her hand to greet someone. She had that particularly surprised, pleased look when coming across someone at a party. The look was always the same, even if she had seen the same person that very afternoon someplace else. Then he saw the expression in Casey's eyes as he looked up at Tom from the bed. They were the eyes of a hurt animal, slowly going out of focus. He saw Casey turn his head, slowly and carefully, to the wall. This image kept coming back and coming back. Tom could not get rid of the idea there was something hurt and, at the same time, accusing in the eyes. He saw the image of Mavis walking away from him, hugging herself, head down and crying, that night in the Square. Then he saw Casey's eyes again, and the whole image suddenly swooped and pulled away to the left. Tom sat bolt upright and looked out the windshield. They were just coming down the last hill of Connecticut. Then he saw Casey, through the windshield, slowly turning his head away. Tom snapped on the radio, and instantly there was loud, cheap music. John threw him a glance.

"You look white," he said.

Tom said nothing. He knew John would not press the matter.

It was a little after three when they reached the house on East 70th Street. John drove the car across the sidewalk, nosing it up to the garage doors, and stopped, letting Tom get out. He said he would bring the luggage up in the elevator from the garage. Tom went directly up to his room, without even asking Mary, who opened the door, for his mother. He flung himself on the bed and closed his eyes. He felt better. The images did not reappear. Within a few minutes he heard the elevator and got up. John was still wearing his driving gloves. Together they brought the luggage into Tom's room, and, after John went back downstairs, Tom unpacked by himself.

The Betancourts were a wealthy family. They belonged to that class of people who had their city residences in those few blocks of New York referred to as the Upper East Side. Its territorial limits were Central Park and Fifth Avenue on the West, Lexington Avenue on the East, 57th Street on the South, and 86th Street on the North. Park Avenue was its core. Most of these people had primary residences in other parts of the world but kept apartments or houses in town for the winter season. They made up their own society, and there were societies within the single society. The Betancourts belonged to the cream. Although they were not descended from early founders, they were considered an old American family because they became rich and conspicuous soon after their arrival. The first Betancourt immigrant, in 1817, fished in Chesapeake Bay, and, by keeping his belt tight, succeeded in buying a small commercial schooner which he plied between Washington and New York. Within a remarkably few years, he was able to buy a larger schooner which he used for whatever trade was favorable. In 1850 he had three ships plying between the East Coast United States and Panama, taking people on the first leg of their journey to the California gold fields. His son became a lawyer and settled in New York, and each succeeding generation took to the law as well. It seemed there had always been a Betancourt law firm in the financial district. The members were in on everything. Each time there was an important railroad dispute, or shipping dispute, they were called in as counsel. They always took their fees in the stock of whatever company was involved, rather than cash, providing a convenience for the company and an increase in capital for themselves. They were always asked to sit on the various boards, and, while serving with distinction, were also able to gain the best intelligence from the confidential movements and plans of the companies. It was a splendid way to keep up with what was going on in the financial world. The Betancourts had always guided their fortunes with shrewdness, foresight, and caution. Their wealth was not momentary or superficial, but rooted deep in the worth of American business. It was not dependent merely upon large annual incomes, but upon ownership of a proportion of American business. Wars and depreciations made only a momentary difference; as American business suffered or gained, the Betancourts suffered and gained, but under any given circumstances they were wealthy in proportion to the rest of the world. The average American millionaire was considered second-class, in this society.

Tom had virtually the whole third floor of the town house to himself. His room was large, with high ceilings, and a fireplace, comfortable chairs and a desk, with three windows overlooking East 70th Street. The house was between Park and Madison Avenues, a pleasant side street still bordered by a few trees and attractive private houses. There were handsome fan lights over the doors of most. In the Betancourt house, the library, drawing room, dining room and kitchen were on the first floor, the principal bedrooms on the second, Tom's large room on the third, and three smaller guest rooms behind it. These were used mostly for his school friends, when they came to stay with him during holidays. The servants had their quarters on the fourth floor. For the most part, they went up and down by the elevator, rather than the stairs. Tom always used the stairs.

His mother had done well with the house. It had been built as a town house in the early part of the twentieth century, and she had been able to modernize it and make it livable without sacrificing any of its dignity, or touch of formality. The house existed as a proper snare: only the people who were used to a touch of formality were comfortable in it; all others were nervous in it and quickly escaped. This saved Mrs. Betancourt quite a lot of bother when it came to making up her guest lists.

Tom knew he would be expected down for dinner. He always was, the first night home. Therefore he spent the latter part of the afternoon in hanging his suits, and putting his socks and things away in the bureau. He put his books on the shelves in their exact places. There was nothing left for the servants to do.

A half hour before starting down, he showered and dressed for dinner. Just as he was getting out of the shower, the house phone on his desk buzzed. He knew it would be John. They had had an arrangement for years whereby John would always call at this time to tell him who would be there for dinner. It provided him with an opportunity to escape, if it looked uncomfortable.

John's husky voice said, "Hey, stupid."

"Yes, Sir."

"Clive just arrived. You want to bow out? I can tell Mary."

Tom considered it. "I can't. This is my first night home. They know I'm here, don't they?"

"Of course."

"Thanks anyway, Johann. I'm stuck."

He put on his dark blue suit, white shirt, tie, and black shoes. It was regulation. More than regulation, he had a distaste for what he called expressive clothing. He felt dark blue expressed nothing.

When he felt he was presentable, he went downstairs to the first floor. He stopped at the library door, which was slightly ajar. He had heard his name mentioned, and knew he should not enter if they were talking about him. Life had made him circumpsect about doors.

He had heard his mother say, "Tom will be here for supper. I hope you don't mind."

"Why should I mind?"

Tom could tell from their voices Clive was at the bar mixing drinks, and his mother was speaking to him from somewhere near the fireplace. She was speaking the louder. He could hear the clinking of the ice against the glass as Clive shook the cocktails.

His mother said, "Tom was born on the coldest night in January. You don't suppose that has anything to do with it, do you?"

Tom turned away from the door.

He heard his mother say, "I know dogs and horses born in midwinter can bear the cold much better, as if they were that much more cold-blooded."

Tom went across the hall into the drawing room. There was one light on, near the principal easy chair. On the table near the chair he saw a cigarette box,

51

and, going to it, took a cigarette. It was the first cigarette he had had in a long time. He smoked infrequently. He believed it hurt his wind for tennis, but now that did not matter. Besides that, he did not care for the taste of tobacco too much. He could smoke or not smoke; it was never any problem for him.

As far as he could remember, his mother's affair with Clive had been going on for the better part of eight years. Nobody seemed to care too much. Certainly he did not. His mother would kiss him on the cheek after supper and say she was going out with Clive. He was a frequent dinner guest and attended all their parties. He was Vice-President of a bank downtown, and Tom thought his father rather liked him. They belonged to the same clubs and even played handball together. Whatever understanding everybody had come to had been established a long time ago. If there had ever been any emotional crisis involved, they had made peace quite by themselves, and it had never showed. Tom doubted there had ever been a crisis. The situation had been going on eight years and it had never gotten in the way. At least no one could say his mother was flighty.

He turned on more lights in the drawing room and walked around it as he smoked his cigarette. His mother had several Cézannes in the room. She had gotten them to blend in with the dignity of the room nicely. She was a bit of a bug on Cézanne. Over the years she had developed a valuable collection. The museums were always after her for it. Tom marveled, as he finished his cigarette, that she had been able to hang paintings, in which the subjects were apt to slop over on each other, in a room in which nothing slopped over on anything. Everything in the room was precise, functional, and handsome. It was seldom used.

When he entered the library, Clive stood up and

shook hands. Tom noticed he was having difficulty focusing, and presumed Clive was slightly mulled. Experience had taught him people usually were before dinner. His mother stood up and held out her arms, as if expecting him to run into them.

"Sweetie," she said. "Just as handsome as ever."

He kissed her on the cheek, and said, "Mother."

Clive immediately put a martini in Tom's hand, and they all sat down. There was seldom anything more to it than that. Tom had seen the expression on his mother's face she always used when greeting people. He must remember to sneak a snapshot of it.

Clive said, "Well, how's the tennis?"

"Smashing." Tom looked at his mother. "Are you well?"

"Perfectly well, thank you. Your father is due back tomorrow, on a late plane. He's in Venezuela. Do you remember Mister Francini?"

"No," Tom said, "I don't."

"He's with Mister Francini," his mother said.

Tom and his mother were sitting in chairs more or less aimed at the fireplace. It was a big fireplace but it only had a little fire in it. Clive was sitting on the footstool, facing them both. He was in the posture of a person much younger than himself, but that was to be expected. Tom had already characterized, in his own mind, this New York society as someone forty-eight trying to be thirty-five. Everyone loved youth, except in the flesh. It was a constant marvel to him how these people, the friends of his mother and father, could eat all the wrong foods, drink daily, starting before lunch, if not earlier, and still give an impression of youth. He knew the way one cigarette would slow him down on the courts next day. The impression of youth must mean a great deal to them, he thought. He found it all rather silly.

His mother said, "Isn't he the handsomest boy you ever saw, Clive?"

Tom knew they were both uneasy with him. Clive was just drunk enough to say something.

"Yes," Clive said, quite as if Tom were not in the room. "But I still can't see how he could ever be your son, Melissa."

"Why, whatever do you mean. Of course he's my son. Do you think I would have a son who wasn't handsome and perfect?"

Clive snorted. "Perfect."

Tom could tell he was suffering from something: either a strange emotion, or heartburn; he could not be sure which.

"He just isn't lovable," Clive said.

"Of course he's lovable. How you talk."

"You're warm, Melissa," he persisted, rolling slightly towards her on his hams. "You've always been a warm person. How could you have a son who is so icy-cold?"

"Clive, do stop it. This is Tom's first night home and he's been through a time of it."

Clive was staring at Tom as if at an animal in the Central Park Zoo. Tom was returning his stare, without much interest.

"Tell me, Tom." Clive leaned forward on the hassock, to impress his seriousness upon him. "Do you love your mother?"

Tom looked over at her. She was sitting up like a puppy hoping for a biscuit, but not really expecting to be given one.

Tom said, "No, I don't think so."

Clive said, "Oh, my God."

"You asked the question," Tom said quietly.

Tom had had his mother on the carpet before. Once before he had calculated their relationship. He had measured the interest they had had in each other, and even then discovered no very real feeling for her. He told the truth, again not because it was a discourtesy, but rather because it was the truth. Tom could never breach his own courtesy, but in this case he could credit it to Clive's having asked the question. It was entirely improper. Clive was not to assume responsibility for him. His mother would have been surprised by any other answer.

"You're a bloody murderer," said Clive.

His focus went on him and, for a moment, Tom worried that Clive might vomit. Clive stood up with difficulty, turning away to lean his arm on the mantelpiece.

"Your mother has told me what happened at school. To tell the truth, I'm shocked."

"She can tell anyone she likes," Tom said, annoyed that Clive felt his feelings would make a difference to him.

His mother said, "Clive, I shouldn't have told you. You're drunk."

"I am not drunk," he said, turning around. "I'm shocked. How can a son of yours be so Goddamned, bloody, murderously cold? Tell me," he said again, more loudly. "Do you love your mother?"

"No, I don't."

Clive put his hands to his temples.

"You're taking all this rather personally, aren't you?" Tom asked.

Clive sat down on the hassock again, almost collapsing; but, Tom noticed, he ended up in the same youthful position as before.

"I feel towards you Tom, as I would towards a son." Clive was trying to look sincere and not burp at the same moment. He had had a son of his own once and had never paid any particular attention to him. "This

55

thing you have done is outrageous: to let your best friend die by his own hand. It makes you seem inhuman. Positively inhuman."

"Perhaps," said Tom.

"Do you love your mother?" said Clive. "Just tell me that. Do you love your mother at all?" His sincere, sweaty, puffy face was pathetic.

Tom put his glass down and leaned forward.

"You know, Clive," Tom said gently. "If I loved my mother, or had any feelings at all for her, you would have been dead eight years ago."

He saw his words sink in slowly.

Clive stood up rather uncertainly and put his glass down on the mantelpiece. He leaned over and kissed Melissa on the forehead.

"I hope you don't mind, but I'm not staying for dinner. I don't feel well."

"That's all right, Clive. Tom and I will manage."

He looked over at Tom. "I'm afraid I haven't been much help."

"That's all right, Clive. You run along."

She took his hand and patted it.

It was the first time Tom had seen Clive act out of line. Clive had always been the figure of propriety, fitting into the life of the family beautifully. He was very sensitive as to which subjects were to be brought up and which ignored. He had always been smiling and gracious, laughing at people's jokes, glad to see people, glad to have a drink with them, sorry to see them go. He had never been outwardly personal with anyone in the house. He had never pretended a responsibility for Tom, but had always treated him simply as a friend of a friend. Tom could never stand to have anyone presume responsibility for him. It was simply that tonight Clive had had too much to drink. He would never have done it, otherwise.

In a few minutes, Mary came to the door and announced dinner. Since Clive left they had been sitting without a word to say to each other.

"We'll be right in," his mother said. "Oh, Mary?—"

Mary had started back towards the dining room.

"Yes, ma'am?"

"There will only be two for dinner."

Mary looked at Tom and winked.

He winked back at her, grinning.

Five

After the main course had been served and Mary had disappeared into the pantry, his mother said, "Tom, do you believe in God?"

He was just putting peas into his mouth, and he finished the motion.

"Does it matter?" he asked.

"I think it does." She put a piece of lamb chop in her mouth and chewed it thoughtfully. "At least I think it ought to."

"I've never given it much thought," he said.

He had never thought of it at all.

"Do you remember Doctor Benton?" she asked. "He's over here in Saint Luke's."

"No."

"Well you should. I bought some papyrus for him."

"Papyrus?"

"Yes. There were some particular papyrus over in Egypt he wanted. Is it papyrii?—Anyway, I bought them for him although I don't know why. They will never be able to leave the Egyptian Museum in Cairo. Doctor Benton thought it would be nice to have Saint Luke's name on them as owner."

Tom did not ask how much this dubious charity had cost the family. Although he was the heir apparent, he really did not feel it was any of his business. He was pretty sure his father would have been able to write the expense off as a valuable tax deduction. Losing money these days was frequently harder than making it.

"Anyway, papyrus quite beside the point, you wouldn't mind if we had him for lunch tomorrow."

"Does that mean we would have to have fish?"

"I suppose it does. Tomorrow is Friday."

"I would rather have a steak for lunch than the minister."

"You don't mind seeing him, do you?"

"Of course not. I'm always courteous to your friends."

"I thought he might be able to help."

"He might."

"Tuesday, then. Tuesday is a good, safe day. I think you'll find him very nice. Everyone believes him an intellectual, although that's rather hard to tell, isn't it. I mean why would he care about papyrus if he weren't?"

"Why, indeed."

"Joan—that's Mrs. Robbins. You remember Mrs. Robbins, don't you?"

"No."

"Well, anyway, Mrs. Robbins says you can always tell an intellectual because he is interested in something no one else cares about. Honestly, she can be quite funny."

"A scream."

They ate in silence then, Mary bringing around the platters again. Tom ate quite a lot. He had not eaten well since Sunday, and the martini had whetted his appetite. It was seldom he had allowed himself a drink. The nausea of the afternoon had completely passed, and he dug into his food with something near enthusiasm. At the same time, it would not have mattered much to him if he had not eaten for two more days. His mother noticed him eating heavily. She had stopped long before she wanted to.

"Perhaps what you need is a woman," she said.

"I've had a woman."

"Have you? Well, I'm glad to hear that. Do you enjoy it?"

"Immensely."

"I'm glad to hear it. I've been rather worried, frankly. It's nice to know you have some blood in you."

"Lots of it," he said. "Bloody Betancourt they call me. You've heard them call me that."

"Yes, I have," she said.

"Would you excuse me?"

They were just finishing, and he made the first move to leave the table.

"What about your coffee?"

"I'll have it somewhere else."

"All right," she said, getting up. "I guess I can have coffee by myself. There's a television play on tonight with Anna Maria Alberghetti. She has such a sweet voice. I was so sorry to hear she had gone to Las Vegas."

She came to the front door with him.

"Won't you need a coat?"

"Perhaps," he said. "But I won't miss it."

"Be sure and be here tomorrow. Your father will want to see you. Tom," she called.

He had his hand on the door and was just beginning to open it.

"Kiss me," she said.

He leaned over and kissed her on the cheek. She threw her arms around his neck, hugging him and kissing him. He could smell her toilet water, just faintly.

"Whether you love me or not," she said. "I love you. Tom, don't you love your mother even a bit?"

60

He freed himself, gently.

"Don't be silly," he said.

Outside the night was cool and a little damp. He turned up the collar of his suit coat and walked east on East 70th Street to Third Avenue and then walked north to 83rd Street, turning right towards Second Avenue to an old brownstone in the middle of the block. From the street he could see lights on in the top storey, and he knew Sarah was in. Tom knew she was too strapped financially for any unnecessary expense. Tom knew almost everything about her.

They had met at an all night party in Greenwich Village more than a year before. They had gone into a dark corner, from which they could barely hear the jazz recordings, and she had told Tom all about herself. She had talked for a long time. Tom had merely sat and listened, encouraging her occasionally with a smile.

She had come East a few years ago, sure she had a promising career as a fashion model. Everyone in South Dakota had encouraged her. She admitted everyone thought her the prettiest girl in the community. She took this apartment on East 83rd Street which was just on the fringe of what might be termed the respectable area. Although it was only a twelve by twenty studio apartment, the price was steep. But that had not bothered her too much. She had been sure she would not be there too long. Her modeling would have her on Park Avenue in no time.

However, she found that getting a job modeling was a job in itself. She told Tom all her woes the first night they met. Everyone seemed to have all the models anyone could need. She tried all the agencies. She passed herself off as an actress to the television studios, but they would not even test her. New York was

61

full of hungry young people with better than average ability in one direction or the other and no one really cared. She worked in a restaurant for a while, and then sold perfume at Macy's.

She explained to Tom a lot of her difficulty was caused by her own confusion. She did not know what sort of a model she wanted to be. One day she would be convinced the-girl-next-door type suited her. But the next day she would be certain she was more femme fatale. She went from one extreme to the other, laughing at herself while she did so. The result of her trying to be two different types at once was that she was apt to be full in the face and gaunt in the chest. Her waist was narrow from all her sitting up exercises, but she was a bit thick in the ankle. Basically, she was an attractive girl. But she just could not look gaunt enough to be a good fashion model, no matter how hard she tried. She would starve herself and go without sleep and let her hair hang limp, yet she could not lose the bloom of South Dakota. Despite all that, she thought she had done well in her chosen profession. In the previous year she had made a little over four thousand dollars from modeling alone, which was almost as much as she could have made working on a regular basis at Macy's.

Tom found her frankness rather amusing. That first night he had squeezed her hand, given her an understanding look, and, taken her home. He had dropped in on her frequently since then.

Tom climbed the stairs to the brownstone and rang her bell in the vestibule. She unlocked the catch without asking who it was. He went up the dark stairs, noticing the pervasive odor of cabbage. She was on the landing of the top floor, waiting for him.

"So it's you, Tom," she said. "What are you doing in town?"

She was glad to see him.

"I came back from school," he said.

She led him into her apartment. She was dressed in black leotards and a black turtle neck sweater. She was really quite cute. She stood in front of him inside the door, with her hands behind her back.

"I know what you want," she said.

"You're right."

He kissed her.

They went into the apartment. It was obvious she had been reading. The only light on was the light over the stuffed and covered chair, and there was a book lying face down on the arm. Tom looked at it. It was a paper covered book on the Japanese No plays.

"Right now?" she said.

He sat in the chair. "Do you have any coffee?"

"Instant." She went into the recessed kitchenette and turned on the hot plate by pulling an electric light chain overhead. "That's all right?"

"Perfect."

She put the water on and came back to plump in his lap.

"I'm so glad you're back," she said. She ran the palm of her hand down the side of his nose and followed his jaw bone. "You're so beautiful and I love you so."

"You do?" he asked.

She got up and poured the hot water and instant coffee into the cups, bringing them back to him.

"There. That didn't take long."

She sat on the floor to drink her coffee, leaning against his legs. They drank it in silence and she looked up at him between his knees and smiled. He bundled her up in his arms and carried her to the day bed, which did double duty as a divan.

She was not in the business. Tom knew there was

very little such business in New York. There were one or two houses here and there, but they were mostly for out-of-towners, if they could find them. The bars in New York served the function of giving people something to drink while they waited for the perfect match. If the perfect match did not come along during the evening, which was unlikely, the bar sent them home a little drunk. Tom thought of prostitution as a quaint old institution, as out of date as the hobble skirt. After centuries of women believing they were doing something for mankind, someone told them that women enjoyed it, too, and every one of them believed it. Prophylactics made them more willing and eager as well, although they did lessen the thrill. People could have intercourse and enjoy it, openly and without restraint. No one was ever the worse for it, as long as no one let his emotions get in the way.

Tom was always certain of his emotional standing with Sarah. The amount of emotion she had to put into the love act was important to him. He had thought consciously about it. She did not hesitate to say she liked Tom better than anyone she had known. She said it sincerely, and he believed her. She loved running her hand over the smooth skin of his shoulders, digging her fingers into his muscle. There was not an inch of fat on Tom, and he was proud of the ease with which he handled himself. He knew she was reacting to him, strongly and personally.

He knew she was a little afraid of him, too. He was too perfect: gentle, passionate, and tender. He tried to guide her, and to complement her every move. He was slow and completely controlled. He let her know what was happening to her at every moment, and she was driven into ecstasy by the precision of his motion. He made love as if he were threading beads on a string. It was a simple act, which consumed him; but there was no

64

real feeling. When he was through, he recovered immediately. Any sweat that was on him was usually hers. He knew this fact, too, surprised if not frightened her.

She had said that she felt if he ever let himself go the way that might be natural for him, he might be unbearably savage. She frequently mentioned this, looking up at him as he sat cross-legged on the bed looking out at the room.

She lay still for a moment.

"Tom what are you thinking of?" she asked.

"Nothing. What should I be thinking?"

"I don't know," she said. "Can I comfort you?"

"I'm comfortable."

She reached her hand out and touched his ribs. She felt for fat or a softness and found there was none. Her prodding did not disturb him.

"Tom," she said. "Do you love me?"

"No."

"Have you ever loved anyone?"

He thought. "No. I don't think so."

"People do love, you know."

"It seems rather a waste of effort," he said.

"Loving you is a waste of effort."

He came down to her, lying flat on his stomach beside her. "I'm sorry," he said. "I love making love to you."

"Yes, but you don't love me."

"Of course not."

"Why of course not?"

He sighed and put his nose against her arm.

She waited for an answer, but received none.

"Tom," she said. "Someday you're going to have to get married."

"Why."

"Because everybody does. You won't love your wife,

because you don't have it in you to love. To truly love."

"So?"

"So someday some girl is going to have to propose to you." She sat up and leaned across his back rubbing his neck with her hand. "Tom: will you marry me? Oh, Tom. Please."

"Why do you ask?" he said.

"Because I love you. I love watching you and touching you and making love to you. I think about you and pray for you. I have something human beings call love, Tom. Can't you understand it?"

He thought. His eye looked up and down the sheet where she had been lying.

He said, "No."

She lay down again, her elbow hitting his nose.

"Just leave the money on the bureau," she said.

"Listen to me," he said. "Love is a weakness. Human beings can have it. When you love, you are vulnerable."

She turned to him, leaning on her elbow. "Vulnerable to what?"

He thought, still canvassing the sheet with one eye.

"Hurt," he said.

"Oh, my darling, have you been so hurt—"

She began to fondle his head, but he sprang up and sat on the edge of the bed. He sat there for a moment, his arms out straight, his hands on the mattress. She watched him, waiting to see what he would do. He lifted himself off the bed using only his hands, and in one smooth, clean motion came to his feet on the floor. He began to dress.

"Are you going?" she asked.

"Why not?"

His tone was civil.

"Will you come again?"

In her voice there was the fear she had said too much.

"Of course," he said.

He sat on the bed and put on his shoes. Leaning over, he kissed her on the cheek and, standing up, put on his coat. She was still sitting on the bed.

"Good night," he said.

She said, "Good night."

He closed the door, leaving her in her room, and whistled as he went down the stairs.

Six

The next morning was gray and cool. It was one of those wet, windy days that make up most of the beautiful springs the poets talk about. Tom dressed and was in the dining room at eight o'clock. Ever since he was a small boy he had obeyed the house rule of being down for breakfast at eight, regardless of what else might have been going on. He could miss any meal, or have it in his room, except breakfast. Coming down to it on time was only fair to the cook, whoever she was that week. Even when he was away at school or on vacation, he got up early and went to where breakfast was being served at eight o'clock, even if no one else was ready for it. It always annoyed Tom to be a guest in a house that arose late as a matter of course. He had never slept beyond seven-thirty in his life.

Immediately after breakfast, he put on his scarf and gloves and walked south on Madison Avenue. He was looking for a pet shop. It was still before nine, and the streets were filled with people on their way to work. He stopped more than once to take pictures. They were uniformly well dressed, and there were thousands of them. They were all carrying umbrellas and wearing raincoats as if they all had heard on the eight o'clock news that it would be raining when they came out of their offices at five. This was the district where most of the important advertising agencies, fashion designers and exclusive dress shops were. Everyone was hurrying, in all directions, and they all looked very important. Tom got that impression of youth, again, although looking closely at the people he discovered there were only a few under forty. They were all slim and quick-stepping. Most of the men had deep tans, although it was early spring, and short haircuts. Very few of them were gray. He noticed the women most, as they bounced out of cabs, hurried along the sidewalks, and swished in and out of the revolving doors of the various buildings. They all had lovely legs and trim ankles and were slim in the waist. They gave an impression of being extraordinarily broad-shouldered, however, and their faces were apt to be the most peculiar shade of orange. No matter how their hair was set, their faces looked quite hard and the skin below their eyes was strangely heavy. He thought of these faces as masks, and he wondered if he could spend a lot of mornings and noon hours down here taking close-ups of the various masks. They might be amusing, seen in quick succession.

At 57th Street he turned west to Fifth Avenue and walked north. Finally, near 62nd Street he found a pet shop. There were cocker spaniel puppies in the window, and they all looked healthy and bright-eyed. He went in and spoke to the proprietor and, after going over the puppies very carefully, chose one. The dog was about three months old and very playful. He had intelligent brown eyes, a happy disposition, and the proprietor assured Tom he had come from champion stock. Tom paid a hundred and twenty five dollars for him. The proprietor very kindly provided Tom with a leash, as a gift of the house, but the dog did not take kindly to it. Once on the sidewalk, he backed up on his haunches and sat down, terrified. It was the first time he had been on the street, and, although he may have spent the last week in the window of the shop looking out at the people going by, he got quite a different perspective from a few inches off the sidewalk. He looked at the legs and feet flashing by him apprehensively and did his best, tugging against the string, to get back into the shop. Tom took pictures of the puppy cringing against the black enamel baseboard of the building. He tried tugging him along, but it would not do. The dog was terrified and Tom had to carry him.

Tom had wanted a puppy for some time. Ever since his cocker spaniel had died, years before, he had been aware of a vague yearning for the sort of love he and his dog had had for each other. There had been a mutual trust and understanding between them he had never since seen repeated. He knew it was ridiculous to allow himself this wistfulness over a puppy, but he had never been able to shake it. It had stuck with him for years. It was inexplicably sentimental of him. Laughing at himself had done no good whatsoever. At first he made bravado jokes about the dog's death, saying he had expired just before his license, but it did not help a bit. The mourning for his dog continued, and with it, a very real yearning to have the dog replaced. He had to have another puppy.

He had tried to analyze this weakness for dogs. Years afterward, when he found himself still sorrowing over the death of his dog, he insisted upon finding out the truth of this love. Tom had to have all emotional relationships clearly stated in his mind. He figured that something had happened between himself and people. A dog's love was one he felt he could trust. This had brought him many times to say he preferred animals to people. The dog had been free with his affection, following Tom here and there, jumping into his lap, kissing him in a most outrageous manner. Tom loved it. The dog had never concealed his love for Tom. Never once had he held a grudge or turned his back on him. His love was never cool or distant and any harm that came from too much intensity was easily rectified. When Tom paid too much attention to him, allowing him to get a little spoiled, it was a simple matter to set the dog down again. A stern word, or a flick of the newspaper on his tail would fill the dog with caution and virtue. This sort of thing was not possible between people. Tom thought a dog's love for his master beautiful. He wondered if he had grown beyond such love.

Shortly after Tom got back to the house on 70th Street it began to rain. It was a gentle, spring rain that would keep up forever. He took the puppy to his room and proceeded to teach him who was master in no uncertain terms. He had decided to call the dog Princeton, for some reason or other. He had bought some biscuits and other dog food on the way back to the house and by first speaking firmly to the puppy, then coddling him, he succeeded in making him nervous and confused. He had a rolled up newspaper which he sometimes twitched at the puppy, with the desired effect. The dog became terrified. He did learn to react to his master, however, and that was all Tom wanted. Simply by patience and perseverence on his part, and patience and forebearance on the part of the puppy, Tom had him responding to his name and sitting fairly regularly on command by noontime.

Tom spent most of the afternoon reinstalling the hi-fi set in his room. It was a terribly complicated job. The way he had it arranged each section had to be placed just so. Princeton looked on uncomprehendingly but with great interest. His desire to help was immediately manifest when he learned how to pull out plugs which had just been put in and proceeded to do so with great glee, scampering around the bed when Tom tried to catch him. Soon he tired of that game, though, and found a good insulated wire to chew on which sparked in his mouth when Tom set the contraption on. He howled, of course, and Tom had to scoop him up and comfort him in the chair. Princeton moaned and carried on as long as the good treatment lasted, looking up at Tom in the most blatantly seductive manner. Tom finally brushed him onto the floor and taped up the spoiled wire.

The hi-fi set took most of the afternoon, and after that came another lesson for Princeton. The puppy was not half as afraid in the afternoon session. He had learned he could please his master (and thus win a biscuit) by remembering what the orders meant, and by reacting to them instantly. Tom wanted to be obeyed immediately, quite forgetting the puppy's need to cogitate. There was a momentary confusion between the words "Princeton" and "sit," but that was quickly dispelled by a few switches with the newspaper. Tom was endlessly patient. He did not let up until the puppy was staggering with sleepiness.

At five-thirty Mary brought his supper on a tray. He was having an early supper because there was to be a dinner party that night for a few of his mother's friends and the staff would be busy with that. His mother had told him at lunch that if he were to come he would make the party thirteen. Tom was really glad to be let off; he hated those parties with a passion. He had often wondered, though, as he was growing up, exactly how many guests his mother really had for these dinner parties. She always said twelve, and he would always make thirteen. Once or twice he had been tempted to go down to the dining room just before the people came and count the places set, but he had never done so. He had never even looked in when he happened to be downstairs and could see through the corner of his eye the gleaming glassware already set in the dark dining room. He knew there might be twelve places set, or fourteen, or ten. He knew it did not matter; he was being foolish about the literal truth. He sometimes thought it was his love for the literal truth that made people think him cold and exacting.

He knew his father would not be at tonight's dinner party, either. He was due at Idlewild at nine-thirty and John would go out in time to meet him. Clive would be there. Clive always went over well at these parties. He had realized a long time ago that banking was something no one wanted to hear about so he listened to other people talk about insurance. He was always a hit. Not being the host, there was never any reason for him to get in anyone's way. Yet he was useful mixing drinks and sitting at the head of the table. Mrs. Betancourt's dinner parties invariably went smoothly, and many of her guests were always surprised how much they had picked up about Cézanne during the evening.

Tom had his chicken sandwich and milk in his room, and then sat awhile listening to the hi-fi and looking out the window. The rain looked silvery coming down at an angle under the street lights, and the black top of the road shone as if under glass. He listened to Errol Garner's *Concert by the Sea* and then a recording made by the Harvard Band. When they played the *Stars and Stripes* he realized he had gotten sleepy and woke up Princeton and dragged him out for a walk. He went down in the elevator to the garage, and out that way. It saved his bumping into the dinner party, for which he was not dressed.

He was wearing only a sport jacket and slacks and he got drenched immediately. Princeton plodded along after him, his nose almost bumping against the sidewalk. Tom led him out to Fifth Avenue and they walked down the boulevard sidewalk under the trees all the way to the Plaza. The trees of Central Park, with their slick and shining bark, looked cold and austere behind the gray stone wall. No one else was out. Taxis filled with people went by. Tom saw several cars pull up at the apartment buildings opposite, the people popping out and hurrying under the canopies into the buildings, holding their collars to their throats. The doormen leapt out with umbrellas at every car that stopped. Tom could see lights in almost all the apartments, sometimes catching silhouettes of people passing back and forth behind the curtains. He saw one silhouette of a man and woman standing at the window, facing each other and talking, each holding a drink. He noticed the male figure had a slight paunch. When he got to the Plaza and turned back, Princeton would have no more of it. He sat down and allowed himself to be dragged several feet. Tom picked him up in his hand and, feeling the puppy shivering, put him under his coat.

He dried Princeton off quite thoroughly when he got back, and then took a warm shower himself. He dressed in his slacks and a sweater and took Princeton up onto his lap.

He then read a short story by Thomas Mann called *Tonio Kröger*. Tom had never thought of himself as an artist, although he enjoyed taking pictures. But he did become interested in this character study of a man who loved intensely, and in secret. Kröger spent years concentrating on his art only to discover, ultimately, that he had closed himself off from the people he loved. He yearned for them. When Tom came to the part where Kröger decided he would give up everything, even his art, to be capable of friendship again, Tom lost interest. He could not believe a man of truly superior accomplishments would yearn for people. He suspected Mann was trying to draw the portrait of a lonely man; if that were the case, Tom had no sympathy for the character. Being alone suggested strength; but feeling lonely was a weakness. If Kröger had such emotion he could not have been truly superior. He belonged with the people.

He had just finished with the story when he heard the elevator. He knew his father was coming up. Tom was stroking Princeton's soft, golden fur. The dog was sound asleep in his lap.

The senior Betancourt was a handsome and distinguished man. He was carrying a little more weight than he should, but he was always tanned and energetic. His hair had grayed in just the right places. His tailoring was always flawless, but nevertheless, staunchly conservative. He was quite successful. Coming out of law school at twenty-five, he had entered his father's New York law firm immediately and was quickly recognized as one of the best brains in the New York Bar. At his father's death, he assumed a senior partnership in the firm of Betancourt, Wilkins, and Campbell and did well with it. He was invited to sit on the boards of many major corporations and had proven himself invaluable, time and again, by using his knowledge of tax law. He made rather a specialty of taxation and was always called to consider the most difficult cases. His briefs were already being studied in both law schools and business schools. They were admired for their clarity and brilliance. He had done well with the family fortune, too, switching from railroads to automobiles to chemicals and electronics just a step ahead of everybody else. He had been a popular president of the New York Bar Association. He was thinking, if he ever had a summer completely to himself, to write a text. He rather fancied leaving a volume behind him called *Betancourt on Taxation*.

Tom did not know much about his father's personal life. He knew his father had never resented Clive, but at the same time, he assumed his father was not too deprived, himself. His whereabouts were usually unknown to Tom. However, each year he had disappeared to California or Honolulu for a month or six weeks, supposedly by himself. There was never any explanation. No one ever called them business trips. His mother would explain to her guests that Tom had run out to California again and that would satisfy everybody. For a while he had kept a yacht in Florida and occasionally would disappear somewhere on that. Eventually, however, he recognized it as more of an expense than it was worth and he gave it up. Tom knew very little about his father, and, as far as he could see, had not suffered from the lack. They had always been on the best of terms.

Betancourt senior pushed the door open and came in.

"Hello," Tom said.

He started to get up, threatening to spill Princeton on the floor; but his father, seeing the dog, put his hand on Tom's shoulder and held him down.

"Has the damn party broken up?"

His father said, "I don't see anybody. I suppose they're all gone." He took a letter out of his pocket and handed it to Tom. "No telling whom we'll find downstairs in the morning."

He went over and stood by the walnut fireplace, waiting for Tom to finish reading the letter.

Tom unfolded it. The paper was heavy and expensive, and the seal of the University was embossed on top. It read:

Dear Mr. Betancourt:

We have in hand a letter signed by your son, Thomas Mathew Betancourt, stating his intention to leave the University and saying he has your permission to do so. We presume he has already left and safely reached his home in New York.

We understand this unusual move is a result of the unfortunate death of his roommate and friend, McKensie Case. As you doubtless know by now, your son summoned the Campus Police for help last Sunday afternoon at about four-thirty, calling them by telephone from his rooms in Horace Mann Hall. When Officers O'Reardon and Brenn arrived they found your son in a state of shock, and the Case boy lying on a bed, having bled to death from the wrists. In his statement to the police, your son admitted having been forewarned of the suicide, and having done nothing either to encourage or discourage it. In fact, while Case was dying, your son remained in another room reading a book, fully aware of the suicide. The police have, in their report to the University, the statement that your son repeated several times that Case "was free," presumably meaning that Case had been free to commit suicide, your son having no right to stop him.

Your son has had an excellent record at the University, in academics and athletics, and was generally popular with the students and the faculty. We had no thought of severing relations with this student, and we would be glad to see him back at any time. Doctor Wilson, the college psychiatrist, was able to spend very little time with him and therefore was unable to come to any conclusions. He did state the belief, however, in his report to the University, that your son might benefit from psychiatric counsel.

If you have any questions, and can come to Boston, we will be glad to see you. All police reports and other records regarding this unfortunate affair will be made available to you.

Respectfully,
Manfred Collier
Dean of Students

"What do you think of it?" his father asked.

"It's factual. I'm not sure I was in a state of shock, though."

His father came away from the mantelpiece. "Would you mind if I stretched out on your bed?"

"No. Not at all."

The thought crossed Tom's mind that he had never seen his father lying down.

"How were things in Venezuela?" he asked.

"Fine. We spent most of the time at Francini's ranch. The flowers were beautiful. By the way, his daughter asked for you."

"That's good. Have I ever met her?"

"I don't think so. I don't think she's ever been up here."

"Well, I hope you told her I was well."

"I did."

His father was gazing at the ceiling, his head tilted far back and his chin up high. He was evidently stiff from the airplane. Tom noticed the way his paunch had collapsed when his father had lain down. It had reversed proportions with the chest. Never having seen anyone overweight lying down, he had not known that happened.

His father said, "Francini is doing well with our investments down there."

"I didn't know we had investments down there."

"We have had. Real estate in Caracas. He's been able to triple our money in some instances. I think I'm going to pull out though."

"Why's that?"

"It looks too unsettled. Those Latins are an emotional lot. You never know when they might start shooting at each other and burning and plundering again. They are very hard to deal with."

He sat up on the bed and looked as if he were about ready to go.

"Look, Tom, about this other matter—" He waved his hand at the letter. "As far as I can see you are not legally guilty of any crime, and you have nothing to worry about."

Tom said, "Otherwise, what do you think?"

"I think you've read quite a lot of Schopenhauer."

Tom smiled. "That's true. I have read a lot of Schopenhauer."

"From what I can see you are expressing an attitude towards existence which is not original. Other men have thought it, and other men have lived up to it. You have the right to try out whatever ideas you think worth the effort."

Tom was playing with the ear of Princeton. The puppy did not seem to mind. He was too thoroughly asleep.

"Do you think I need a psychiatrist?"

"You're not legally insane until there is evidence you don't know right from wrong. That is a silly definition. It has outlasted the period when society thought it knew right from wrong. From your point of view you may have had more right than you know not to have prevented his suicide. To the emotional washerwoman there would be no doubt that you were wrong."

Tom waited, and then he repeated the question. "Do you think I need a psychiatrist?"

"I think everybody needs a psychiatrist. If you want to see one, go ahead. No one will think the worse of you. Do you want to see one?"

"I don't think so."

"Tom, what do you want to do now that you've left the University?"

The image of a small sailing boat with one head in it sailing out of a harbor on a clear day suddenly darted across his mind. Tom was not given to having this sort of image.

"I don't know. Nothing."

"Well," his father said, standing up. "You don't have to do anything. Come downtown with me next week and have lunch with me. Play handball. I can show you off to my friends."

"I'd be glad to."

His father pointed at the dog. "Where did you get that?"

"That's Princeton. I bought him this morning."

"Looks sleepy. Well, goodnight. Tomorrow's Saturday, but I promised to go to Philadelphia. John's picking me up at seven."

Tom heard his father at the elevator. In a moment, he was gone and Tom heard the door to it open on the second floor. He thought it would have been easier if his father had walked down one flight of stairs.

He went to the window and looked out, leaving Princeton in the chair. It was still raining.

Seven

The next week was fairly aimless. Tom made few plans of his own, coming and going to suit the plans of the house. As a matter of course he was always down for breakfast at eight. Each morning he told the cook if he would be in or out for lunch and dinner taking the cue from his mother at breakfast. He always took the hint. He was always in for meals his mother arranged for him and out for parties she arranged for herself. John and Mary were a further help. They would let him know if there were to be a cocktail party that night, which might permanently impair the dinner hour. They would tell him if he might be better off having a sandwich at Mayhew's. Tom had made the mistake when he was younger of coming into the house while there was a cocktail party in progress only to have the matrons slobber over him and the gentlemen drag him into the library there to forget him and leave him to worm his way out. It had always been embarrassing for him. People were invariably much more drunk than they knew and, what's more, apt to run out of conversation before they ran out of gin. The child of the house, in this case, Tom, was instantly seized upon as a conversation piece. They would discuss his attractiveness in the most blatant way, as if he were not there at all. They would ask him about his University and show too obvious approval that he was in the Ivy League. They would ask him about his girls. They would question him specifically about his academic standing. The gentlemen would have to know how many letters he had won, and for which sports. The sickening part of it was that they were not the slightest bit concerned. If he went and hung himself, not even a momentary silence would be noticeable in the room.

Tom hated these parties. Everyone had a right to know everything about him, because they all dearly loved Melissa and Tom was Melissa's son. They all had the right to be maternal towards him, or paternal, as the case might be, even though he might never see them again. Without any doubt in anybody's mind, they all had license to be completely rude to him: prying, condescending, and disgustingly insincere. He was a safe object for their attention at a certain point in their drinking because they felt they need not make even the slightest effort toward sincerity. It was fine for them to have a youth to pore over, for sincerity was such a hard job after the fifth Manhattan; and, youths instinctively liked people. Once, when he was quite young, a woman had fussed over him inordinately and quite intimately, then, turning on him, to the party at large, repeated something he had said in all sincerity, screamed with laughter and called it "cute." This was the sort of behavior Tom had never been able to accept. It infuriated him. However, he learned to deal with such situations. He became adept at turning an affront around. He would be equally prying, condescending and insincere. He would stare at a man's paunch, asking him about his handball, saying, in a happy voice, "One has to keep up one's sports, doesn't one?" With the appearance of complete naiveté, he might ask a woman who had been complimenting him if her daughter were home from college yet. She would turn green. He never let himself be serious. When a banker asked him his plans for the future, he would solemnly answer, "Banking," although he had never considered becoming a banker in his life. Sometimes he would spin a web around the man, giving an expository talk, explaining how much the banking institution had meant to Western society and civilization, concluding with the thought that he had equally considered becoming a stringer of tennis racquets. He even learned how to pose an extraordinarily involved question to an expert, such as a lawyer, and slip away before the man had a chance to collect himself. Tom shunned these parties as if his life depended upon it.

He was a model of propriety the day he met his father downtown for lunch at the Club. With great hellos they marched into the bar. Tom was constantly called upon to meet people. He would shake their hands and be quickly elbowed back. Someone put a martini in his hand, and he drank it. He knew they all expected him to listen to their conversations, deriving education from them. They were all concerned with the big news of the day (some stock had dropped five points), and Tom thought this no more intelligent of them than it was of fishermen to talk about fish or bricklayers about bricks. It was all trivial. Two men turned to him, one winking, the other gripping his elbow, to ask how "the team" would do next year. Tom assured them both that where we were weak on foils we were strong on épée. Neither had waited for his answer.

At lunch, his father talked to him about various clients, and that was interesting. Mr. Betancourt could see clearly and coolly through the people with whom he did business. He knew the faults and weaknesses of each of them. He knew which would back down at the first show of firmness, which would be adamant, though wrong; which could be controlled like a child. All these things were as simple, obvious, and certain to him as a mathematical equation; there was no mystery. Some men had the "stuff," and others had not. Some of them were dreamers and idealists and did not last long. Others provided a good challenge for a quick brain. During the luncheon Tom wondered if there might not be something in this for him, after all. He had never been much interested before. He rather liked the idea, however, of getting personalities down to algebraic formulae.

They had to go back to the office for a while after lunch while Betancourt Senior had a conference, which would not last long. Afterwards, they would play handball.

The men were already there when Tom and his father arrived at the office. There was more handshaking, and all the men were delighted to meet Tom. They squeezed his shoulder and knocked the back of his head. They smiled at him, asking questions which were designed to show familiarity. Most of them fell back upon "the team." The spirit of the locker room prevailed, possibly because Tom was there. They had all been athletes, one place or the other; they had all been young and free. Everyone feels akin to youth; or perhaps everyone simply feels guilty over having lost it. He made a big hit. The office boy, who was about the same size as Tom, quietly looked at Tom as he handed in some papers through the door. It was quite easy for Tom. All he need do was not look bored and everyone believed in him. He was Tom Betancourt's son.

The conference went on for better than an hour. The figure seven and a half million dollars recurred time and again, someone mentioning a new plant in Springfield, Illinois. Each time the topic was about to crystallize, Tom noticed, the commuting problem crept in. None of these gentlemen liked the Pennsylvania

Railroad, the New York Central Railroad, or the New Haven Railroad. The Lexington Avenue Subway was ghastly, and the advisability of getting on at Brooklyn Bridge was discussed. New York taxi drivers were an individual and independent lot, and they were cursed roundly. The food on the airlines was terrible. But after an hour they broke up, shouting at each other as they went out the door what they had decided, no two of them saying the same thing. Everyone promised to send memos to each other, and one or two were going to get up figures. They all forgot to say goodbye to Tom and had to come back to shake hands and tell him to "keep plugging," whatever that meant. It was obviously supposed to mean something, as they all winked and laughed uproariously. After they left, Tom's father had him close the door.

He sat down again behind his desk. "We didn't accomplish a damn thing," he said. "The bastards."

Finally, they went to play handball, and Tom won every point. It did not occur to him to lose. His father flung himself about the court with a monkey's enthusiasm and an elephant's grace. He had assured the boy he would beat him, and there was no doubt he threw his heart and soul into the game. He would make wild stretches and terrific throws, being dismayed that Tom would be able to pick it up and return it without appearing to move. He could not beat the boy's clean smooth stroke and easy grace. He eventually insisted he was going to get one point before he was through, but Tom was playing the game the way he did everything else. He had no thought for his opponent at all. The game was to be well-played and well-won. The mere fact that his father was stamping about, huffing and puffing, and yet not able to get a point was not to be taken into consideration. Tom thought his father should play handball better. Finally, his father insisted they had had plenty of good exercise and must do it again. It was with some annoyance that he mentioned his son was neither out of breath nor sweating. He brought Tom back to the locker room, quite ignoring his suggestion they take a swim.

In the locker room Betancourt was in his element. He padded around in his towel greeting people and asking about this and that. Tom had to come forward and shake hands with all of them, trying his best to keep from staring. He had never seen anything like the incredible rolls of fat. They all stood up for him, to a man, their fat looking better that way, and Tom wondered if this might not be how the custom started. He was sure they would not be so quick to rise for him if they had been belted and vested. Afterward, on the other side of the lockers, Tom's father, whispering to him, exploded the personality each man had tried to project.

Tom did not play handball with his father again. He did go to the gymnasium several times himself, at least three times a week, and took a strenuous two or three hours of exercise. Each day of his life, when Tom arose, he would do eighty push-ups and a few other things, before he took his cold shower. Before dinner, while he was dressing, he would do another eighty, in series of twenties, sitting-up exercises and other things, as they occurred to him. When he went to the gymnasium for exercise he would chin himself twenty or thirty times, twirl himself around on the bars, jump rope and play whatever sport for which he could find a partner. He did all these things with the precision of a musician practicing his scales. He never lost concentration or became bored with it. During this period, when everyone he knew was away at University, he had difficulty finding partners for squash and handball, so he would do thirty, forty or fifty laps up and down the pool. His form was perfect and his stamina endless. He would not have had it otherwise.

Noontime Tuesday, Doctor Benton, the Rector of Saint Luke's, came around for lunch. He, too, had affected the crew-cut and youthful manner, although neither suited him. Left to his own devices, Tom thought he might have been a pleasant, soft-spoken man. As it was, he apparently felt the obligation to be vital, and the strain showed. He was obviously not cut out to be vital. Mrs. Betancourt, using her usual perspicacity, served sherry in the library and eggs Benedict for lunch. They went down very well. Doctor Benton was very glad to meet Tom, and asked after his friend, the college chaplain, whom Tom had never met. He said he had been rather hoping Tom could help him remember the man's name, but Tom had to disappoint him. Doctor Benton knew he had met the man at a convention somewhere. The servant problem prevailed, and, after that, snow removal from the city sidewalks. Thoughts on the papyrus problem came with lunch, Mrs. Betancourt being a little slow to understand the Egyptian government's point of view, but she got it with the melon. She thought the Egyptians frightfully narrow.

Over coffee in the library, she suggested she might leave the two of them alone, but Doctor Benton looked horrified and said he had promised to be at Lenox Hill Hospital at three. What he had to say to Tom would only take a moment.

He said, "Son, your mother has told me of the episode with your roommate at college, and I think I can assure you we all understand. Even the best of us becomes scared. Fear can immobilize one. We all know you would have done something else, if you had had a moment to think about it. Fear is a dreadful thing: positively paralyzing. But it's nothing to be ashamed of, especially for one as young as you. Only a man of true maturity, who has learned from bitter experience to react quickly and properly to crisis, can face fear without being paralyzed by it. We all understand. But I do want to refresh you on one thing: it is one of the basic tenets of our faith that we are our brothers' keepers. You mustn't forget that. What happens to them is important to us. Their pain and suffering are important. So is their despair. You must save them from themselves. You must stop them if they do wrong, even if only to themselves. It is by such a Christian tenet as this that we lead our lives. We know you have not lost sight of it. You could not have lost sight of it and still be Melissa's son. We understand you were unable to act through fear. There can be no other explanation. But, to be a good Christian, you must learn to conquer that fear."

Doctor Benton looked immensely relieved when he was through. He immediately found his hat, mentioning Lenox Hill Hospital, and went to the door. Tom rather liked the man. He had thought out what he was going to say before he came. It suggested exactness to Tom, conscientiousness. Also, the man had not pretended responsibility for him. He had not intruded a bit. He had seen his job as that of assuaging guilt, if there had been any, doing it smoothly and painlessly. He had done precisely that. Tom went to the door with him.

"You must come to service, Tom," Doctor Benton said. He was fixing his scarf. "Lots of young people do come now."

"Yes, sir."

They said goodbye to each other and shook hands. Tom started up the stairs. His mother stood at the bottom.

"Doctor Benton is such a help," she said. "Such a peaceful man."

Tom, from the staircase, said, "It must be a nice life, Mother."

He was perfectly sincere.

The letter from Ellen Case did not arrive until Thursday afternoon. Tom had been out somewhere and found it on his desk on his return. It had been addressed to Mann Hall at the University, and forwarded from there. It was originally postmarked the Wednesday before, which must have been either the day of the funeral, or the day after. Tom rather thought she would have written it the day after. It had been mailed from New Hope, Pennsylvania, and was written in an uneven hand.

Dear Thomas Betancourt:

I loathe you. My brother, McKensie, was a good, happy boy, with every reason to live. He must have had a most corrupt and evil influence working on him. I can only believe that the man who would be callous enough to stand aside and watch with disinterest while his friend bled to death must be the same corrupt and evil man.

I hope you are haunted by his memory. I hope the thought of what you have done makes you destroy yourself. I hope you rot in hell.

Ellen Case

Tom folded the letter and left it on his desk.

He immediately took Princeton in hand and began going over the first early lessons. The puppy was learning well. He would come at the slightest provocation and sit down at the clearing of a throat. He was completely broken to the leash and just beginning to learn the necessity of walking to heel. He was about to learn a great many more things which, unfortunately, he would never be able to use. He was eager to please Tom and win his biscuit.

After a full two hours of working with Princeton, Tom read Ellen's letter again. He took the picture of Ellen out of his desk drawer and looked at it for a long moment before putting them away together.

It was while he was showering for dinner that he decided he had to get to know the Case family. He was not sure how he could arrange it, but he thought spending the summer in Yarmouth, Massachusetts might be as good a way as any. The town was a summer resort and there would be flocks of young people. His being there would be natural. No one would notice one more young man of college age, and he felt sure he could arrange to conceal his identity. He was pretty sure he could work out the details.

He did not know why he wanted to know the Case family. He realized it might be irrational of him. For some reason he was drawn to Ellen Case. He had decided to do it even though he was not sure why he wanted to. He had nothing else to do that summer, anyway.

PART II

Yarmouth

Eight

As usual, in the first week of June, the Betancourt household moved out to Sparrow's Point. It was a large rambling place on Long Island. It was not a formal house, or show-place, as much as a country residence. The gardener kept the grounds spotless, and an aura of charm prevailed, but still the general effect was not breathtaking. The Betancourts had never gone in for the ostentation affected by many American millionaires. Being truly rich, they had learned to be somewhat obscure. The house was a large, brick structure, with wings and chimneys, looking not nearly as large as it really was. It had forty rooms, each one spacious and airy, but anyone seeing a photograph of it might not look twice. It was a rather old place, as American houses go, having been built in the 1890's and added to in the 1920's. Modern luxuries had been provided as the need arose: the swimming pool, tennis courts, and boat houses built according to the needs of each generation. Tom had enjoyed the use of all of them, except when he was away at school in the winter or at camp in the summer. For the most part, they were an athletic family, and always enjoyed the company of athletic friends. It was an enjoyable house to visit. Guests were not obliged to follow the routine of the family (except for breakfast at eight) but could come and go, using the facilities they chose. Tom had never paid much attention to any guests that might be there. He saw them at meals and frequently found that a boat or horse he had planned on using was already in service to them, but for the most part he saw very little of them. He considered them all guests in the same hotel: he was seldom sure of their names and treated them all with a distant courtesy.

When, at sixteen, Tom had been given the Ford convertible and John had taught him the rudiments of driving on the grounds of Sparrow's Point, Tom had had little real use for the car. Having it in Boston would only be a nuisance. There, it was difficult to find parking places, and the University, always having to make peace with the local authorities, urged the students to leave their cars at home. If Tom ever needed to go anyplace, he could always borrow a car, and John transported his luggage back and forth in the Mercedes. In New York, the car was even more useless. Taxis and subways were much quicker. As a result, Tom kept the car at Sparrow's Point. The gardener would start it once a week and drive it around the grounds to keep it in running order. In the three years he had the car, Tom had only been able to put twenty-five hundred miles on it. Today, it was virtually new.

One early June day, when John was not busy with other duties for the family, he drove Tom out to Sparrow's Point. He left Tom there, and Tom went to the garage and drove his own car out. Tom had arranged with the gardener to have it checked over at the garage. It seemed perfectly all right to him, and he drove it right back to New York, not even stopping to go into the house. He did take a swim in the salt water near the boat house, but he had brought a towel out from the city for that purpose. He had been sure he would not be able to find a towel in the house. At Sparrow's Point he had never known where anything was.

Back at East 70th Street, John helped him pack. Tom took one good suit, one pair of slacks and a sports jacket, and the necessary socks and shirts. For the most part he knew he would wear khaki trousers which had become regulation for young men for all but formal occasions. They had replaced white ducks and gray flannels, being of tough material and infinitely washable. He brought sneakers and tennis racquets and bathing trunks, but left his hi-fi and recordings behind. He was not sure what accommodations or arrangements he would be able to make for himself.

Somehow everything fitted into one bag, and next morning he drove off to Yarmouth and Cape Cod. He took Princeton, who found great delight in traveling by car. He loved to stick his nose out the window and have the wind whip his ears back. He would stand with his forefeet on the arm rest, keeping his head out the window for as long as he was in the car. He refused to miss a thing. He stood that way virtually all the way to Yarmouth, which was a five-hour drive from New York.

Tom enjoyed the drive down the Cape to Yarmouth. Route Six was a good road, although the going was a bit slow through Providence. It was his first time on the Cape, and he stopped off at Plymouth to see the replica of the *Mayflower*, and the Rock. The ship surprised him; he could not understand how so many people had spent so much time together in such cramped quarters. He thought it must have been a beastly trip, the people falling all over each other and getting in each other's way. He shuddered at the thought. The Rock was interesting to see; he had always heard about it. The fort seemed small to him and again the thought of so many people living in such a small place struck him as unbearable. They must have found each other dreadful bores. He did not spend much time at Plymouth. His

95

principal reason for stopping was to let Princeton relieve himself.

He knew he would like Yarmouth the minute he drove into it. The idea of the New England chill had always appealed to Tom. He had liked what he had seen of it in Boston. Coming along the road into town he knew instinctively Yarmouth had been able to maintain that chill. The houses were oversized and yet seemed modest behind green trees and hedges. The driveways were all well defined and all the window shades were in order. He could tell some of the houses were only used in the summer. Their windows were shuttered and the grass around them was a little long. But, at the same time, these summer places were substantial, three storeys high and with sizable gardens. Tom knew they would have furnaces in the cellars. There was nothing impermanent about them. To the extent that a summer colony existed, the town was a resort. But there was none of the popcorn-trailer-camp disease, which had affected most resort areas. Driving along the water, he thought he had discovered the reason for the town's being able to resist the onslaught of cheap tourism. The waterfront was not the best.

Tom drove into the town and walked Princeton around. It was early June and only the natives were on the street. He stopped at the hardware store and looked into the grocery store, through the window. At the drugstore he ordered a sandwich and fell into conversation with the woman who served him. She was eager to talk with him and had difficulty looking away. She was forty and rather dumpy. She asked Tom if he were down for the summer, and he replied he would like to find a summer job. She was all too glad to help. Her principal suggestion was that he try the Boat Club, and she explained to him in detail how it had been founded and supported by the summer people. It had a pool, a dock, cabanas, a small club house, and moorings. She said they hired one or two boys each summer, and asked him if he knew Chuck Morrison. Chuck, she said, was the town boy who worked at the pool during the summer, and attended Boston University during the winter. The stories he had to tell about the summer people! Tom said he thought he would try the Club, and asked for directions. She said to ask for a Mister Perry when he got there.

Tom drove out the long road which led to the Club. It was really only a shack with cabanas leading off it in one direction, around two sides of the pool. Below the pool, on the waterfront itself, was the dock, with a small shack on it about the size of a telephone booth. Tom finally found Mister Perry. He gave his name as Tom Mathews. He had an easy time getting a job. The Club needed a waterfront attendant, and Tom assured Mister Perry he could swim and sail. The pay, thirty dollars a week, was fine, and he could start immediately. He could live in one of the shacks which had been built onto the cabanas for the use of the boys. They were of bare wood and were a bit drafty, but they had light. No one would mind Princeton. There were so many dogs around usually that Princeton would never be noticed. It was obvious he was a well-trained dog, anyway. Mister Perry said Chuck would be surprised to meet Tom. He had been looking at Tom and something had struck the man amusing. Finally, he came out with it. Chuck had worked at the pool for two summers, and had always been the big man around the Club. The girls had made a constant fuss over him, and, Perry suspected, that was the principal reason he had come back. He had the pick of dates. He had never had competition.

Perry allowed humorously that Chuck might not be too pleased to see Tom. Chuck was a town boy, the son of the hardware man. He had done well at the local high school, playing football and saxophone, and had been sent up to Boston University. He was one of the few town boys who had made it and was already making a name for himself on the football team. The townspeople were great admirers of his. He was something of a star, and the summer people had taken to him and given him the job at the Club. They invited him into their homes, if there should be a dance, and treated him almost as if he were one of them. The men talked seriously with him about his career, Mister Perry observed. The mothers thought he was a darling. Chuck, right now, was rather pleased with himself, and thought they were all grand people. For the most part, they were rich, but they did not hesitate to treat him as an equal. They had seen his name in the sports pages. There was never any strain.

Mister Perry brought Tom to his room and went out to find Chuck. They would be working together and might as well get to know each other as quickly as possible.

On first glance, Tom thought Chuck a decent sort, but none too brilliant. He was big, and for the most part muscular, but Tom could see that much of his bigness was just pure heaviness. He was redheaded, and his eyes were rather close together, and he had an amiable smile, he looked quite innocent. Tom shook hands with him. Again, he gave his name as Tom Mathews.

Chuck helped him unpack, and was clearly relieved to find Tom was not overburdened with worldly goods. He had noticed the Ford convertible in the driveway and had been curious about it. The khaki trousers, however, satisfied him that Tom was the usual college student working his way through school. Tom told him he was from New York and went to Columbia. He presumed no one in Yarmouth knew more about Columbia then he did. Chuck promised to show him the ropes and introduce him to all the girls. The summer people, for the most part, would arrive in the last week of June, or the first week of July. In the meantime, he and Tom had to lay down the moorings and paint the poolside furniture. He said he was glad Tom was there.

Tom got to know Chuck well in the following weeks. Chuck was full of promise and hope. He believed in things, referring constantly to sex and love and sports. In the evenings, he and Tom would buy quart bottles of beer and sit in one room or the other talking about this and that. Tom drank very little of it. Although both were considered minors under Massachusetts law, Chuck's cousin owned a liquor store and provided him with what he wanted. After two small glasses of beer, Chuck would become convinced he was drunk and begin slurring his words. He was taken up with the thought of being drunk. These bull sessions would last for hours, Chuck doing all the talking. Tom would ask a polite question now and again, not really being interested. Chuck worried about the state of the world. He did not like Communism. He thought there ought to be more religion. He wondered about the existence of Christ. He wanted to get married. He thought the sexual experience must be fine, and freely confessed himself a virgin. Americans have always confused celibacy with morality, Tom thought to himself. Chuck was enthusiastic about the line-up of the Red Sox. He thought Hemingway great. He also liked Daniel Defoe. Tom marveled at him. He had never been exposed to such a person. He thought Chuck the true red-blooded American boy: he was incredible.

During the days they set moorings. Chuck did everything in the most difficult and complicated way. He would never think a thing through before he began, but blunder in, making several false starts. He would always have to get more tools. He would always lift things himself rather than rig a hoist or use a wheelbarrow, bending his knees and keeping his back straight. It was all good exercise, he said, and got him in shape for football. Eventually, he would get himself involved in something, and Tom, with a few clean, simple movements would bring it to a fast, happy conclusion. This always amazed Chuck. He used to make loud noises of incredulity at the quick, easy way Tom would do things.

Chuck talked about the summer girls almost continually as they walked around doing this and that. He mentioned the town girls, too, but let it be understood he had no hope for them. They were not quite in his class. Of the summer girls, he mentioned which had good asses and which had good boobs. He marveled at a good set of boobs, as he called them, and discredited any girl who was without them. He thought sex fine. He never mentioned the Case girl.

Tom asked about her.

"Do you know her?" Chuck asked.

They were standing by the pool, having finished painting.

"I knew someone who knows her. Someone at Columbia."

"She's not here much," Chuck said. "She's usually away somewhere. Her parents do a lot of traveling, and she is usually here only for a week or two at the beginning of the season. She has a nice ass, though."

"How are her boobs?" Tom asked, seriously.

Chuck thought. "Okay," he said. "She had a brother who committed suicide this year at school."

"How do you know that?"

"Everyone in town knows it. He got himself into some affair with another guy at school."

Chuck seemed ashamed at the thought.

"What do you mean, affair?"

"You know what I mean, affair."

Tom was amazed. He could not see how a town could come to this conclusion.

"Do you believe it?" he asked.

"Sure," Chuck said. "I've seen him once or twice here at the pool. He always struck me a little that way."

"He did?"

Tom did not want to seem too surprised, but all the same, he was.

"I think he was a little that way. I believe it."

Tom had the quick image of Casey's eyes looking up at him from the white sheet again, and then slowly turning towards the wall. He remembered the hurt look, slightly accusing. He pictured himself in the doorway, looking down.

Chuck was picking up the paint cans and rags.

"By the way," he said. "Hands off the Case girl."

"Oh?"

"Yes, they're really loaded. There's no room for you or me there."

"Oh," Tom said.

"Not unless you're loaded, too." Chuck had indicated curiosity of this matter before. Apparently he suspected Tom's family might be rich. "You're not loaded, are you?"

"Loaded?"

"I never neard of the Mathews family."

"Of course you never heard of the Mathews family," Tom said. "My father's a lawyer."

Tom knew Chuck would picture twelve thousand a year and a shingle somewhere. Chuck had mentioned a cousin who was a lawyer. He went to court over traffic accidents and drove a Buick.

"Mine's in the hardware business," Chuck said. "But I guess you know that. The Case bitch isn't in our league, boy. Look, but don't touch. There's plenty of ass around here."

"Okay," Tom said, "Leave me some."

Chuck grinned. Tom had made himself thoroughly likeable.

Nine

The first day Tom had free from the Club he went out to find the Case house. He asked directions in the village.

He knew there would be no one there. None of the summer people had arrived.

It was a different looking, modern house at the end of a long peninsula, standing low among the rolling dunes. It was gray, weathered, giving the impression from a distance of utter isolation. The sand forbade any real grass, although there was a type of hardy weed cut rather short surrounding the place. The trees were a scrub pine, which increased the look of desolation. It was windy on the peninsula, and Tom noticed the force of the wind against his car as he drove towards the house.

From a distance, it had appeared to be a low, rambling Cape Cod remodeled to serve as a summer house. He left the car at the end of the drive and walked around. Up close, he discovered the house was radically modern. It was bedded in concrete and steel and had cantilevered lounges and decks on the sea side. The front of the house, although of the usual gray shingle, with low, snug windows, had been designed, in some way he could not fathom, to give an impression of lightness. The house contradicted itself. It was deceptive in that it looked conventional, but at the same time looked as if it might take flight at any moment. Tom remembered Casey's father was an architect.

As he walked around the house, taking pictures of it from all angles, he felt slightly uneasy. He had the feeling it was about to move toward him through the dunes, or slip slowly into the sea. Sighting through the lens, he found himself hoping the house, as a subject, would keep still while it was being photographed.

Before he left, he looked in through a few of the windows. The furniture had been covered with sheets and the rugs rolled up.

He stood by the car a moment, wondering again what there was about the house that made it look about to move. It seemed as able to shift its position in the wind as the sand around it.

Driving back to the Club, he wondered just when Ellen Case would arrive. He found he was eager to meet her. In fact, his entire interest in life at this point was his curiosity about Ellen Case.

The girls who appeared at the Club as the season opened did not interest him. The prevailing age was fifteen and a half, and they were all giggly. Boys were their primary, if not sole, topic of conversation, and Tom was aware that he immediately became the principal subject. They treated him as if he were the handsomest creature they had ever seen. His job, half on the waterfront and half at the pool, kept him in his swimming trunks almost all the time, and the girls made him constantly aware that he had broad shoulders and a thin waist. He heard them whisper to each other that he was quiet and that he had dark solemn eyes which doubtless indicated unspoken tragedy. He knew there was nothing more appealing to young girls than the thought of unspoken tragedy. They all fell in love with him, or rather, suffered from adoration spasms the minute they saw him. He would find them clustered around his Ford convertible. More than once, he found impassioned love notes under his door, all unsigned.

Most of the girls over sixteen were not spending the summer with their families. They had gone off to get summer jobs for themselves, to earn money, to escape their families. They were eager to have adventures and be on their own, and Yarmouth would allow neither. For the most part they had gone to the cities to work as summer replacements in the insurance and banking offices. The girls mentioned a few who had taken jobs as counselors at summer camps, and others who had simply headed across country to get whatever jobs they could on the West Coast. The Club was a family club; but the older children of the families were not there. Summertime for them had ceased being a family affair.

The few older girls who arrived admitted freely they were only there because they had to be. Some of them had failed their examinations and therefore had to spend the summer studying. The rest were needed at home for one reason or another. They professed to be happier at having to stay home once they saw Tom. He learned from Chuck that they were writing to their friends who had gone away for the summer, telling them about him, trying to make them envious. He assumed that they would report how well they were doing with him, what he had said to them, and, more to the point, what he had really meant. Tom knew he was an object of competition among the girls.

Princeton never received so much attention. They knew he was Tom's dog, and cuddled him to exhaustion. Princeton was not used to it, but loved every minute of it. The three months of his life which had been spent with Tom had been exhausting. He was almost full-grown now, and could do any and every trick, upon instantaneous command, that any puppy had ever learned. Mrs. Betancourt had referred to Princeton as the only dog in the city that should be allowed to vote. He was not the usual soft, city lap dog. He had been trained to perfection. He was well-mannered, never getting in anyone's way, and always willing to go through his tricks. He seemed very proud of himself. At the same time, he had the independence of a cat, coming and going upon his own whim. If he chose to greet a stranger, he would do so, allowing himself to be played with and petted, but suddenly stalking off to find something else to do. There was a poodle bitch who came to the club with a fat woman, and each time the bitch entered Princeton would try to strike up a friendship with her. He was excited about her, but his attentions were never returned. Even his frustrated love-life struck the girls as amusing. They loved him. And, every one of them realized he was an excellent way to get to Tom, since he frequently sat with whomever had Princeton when he came up from the waterfront. The girls took care of the dog continually.

Tom dated one or two of the girls, as the whim took him, usually as a double date with Chuck. They would go to the local movie and soda shop and to the local necking place. Tom would neck in the front seat, Chuck in the back. The radio would be on, playing loud thumping music interspersed with heart-to-heart advertisements on storm windows and cigarettes. The music was sentimental and repetitious, all the same rhythm, each record having a different sort of voice distortion. Tom did not care about all that. He had always thought the routine of the date rather a bore, but it was the thing to do in that circle. Chuck thrived on these dates, discussing the merits of the various asses and boobs all the next day. Tom found dating the answer to his own needs; there were no other solutions in Yarmouth, Massachusetts.

All the girls he dated said they were in love with him. He would look at them from his side of the car, his eyes dark and serious, his face expressionless, pretending he was taking them seriously. He understood the statement was part of the game and meant nothing. He observed the girls' frustration with total detachment. He assumed they were concerned with silly problems of morality, important to them, but of no importance to him. He could see them wrestling with their consciences. Through their eyes he could see them go through the stages of wondering if they would sacrifice themselves to him if he should ask, deciding they would, and then wondering if he would ask. He never did. They would then try desperately to stimulate him, to bring him to the point where he might ask, make him feel something akin to what they apparently felt, make him become excited, make him love. He defeated every one of them.

Chuck had a marvelous time. He told them all he loved them, and meant it each time. He told each she was the most beautiful girl in the world, although frequently he got her name wrong. There was nothing savage or intense about Chuck. In fact, he went about things rather like an adolescent. He was all over whichever girl happened to be at hand, charging at her like a regiment of cavalry. After each session he would be in a daze and not able to suppress a silly grin. He always looked foolish. All next day, he would go over it with Tom, insisting much more had happened than had. The truth was, he did not know the difference. Tom always let Chuck prattle on, pretending to take him seriously, too.

Tom did not see Ellen Case until the second week in July. He recognized her across the pool from her picture, and then he heard the girls greet her by name. She was much better looking than he had thought, although by no means beautiful. She had a fine, athletic body, compact and trim, with smooth legs and a flat stomach. Her breasts were fine, under her bathing suit, but by no means outrageous, and her shoulders were square and small. She was a light blond, with blue eyes and a long neck. She moved with a happy certainty. It was plain to Tom, even from across the pool, that she would know her way around a tennis court.

He did nothing to meet her then. He did not want to appear too eager. He was afraid that she might recognize him. He knew that he had been in photographs with Casey, and was not sure if the Cases might not have seen one. There might even have been a photograph of the two of them together sent back in the trunk. By and large, though, he had been the one taking the pictures and, therefore, had been in few of them. He wanted Ellen Case to get used to seeing him around before he made her acquaintance, so that she would have a chance to recognize him from a distance, if she were going to at all.

His duties were to ferry the people to their boat moorings, to teach sailing to the children as well as water skiing from the club speedboat, and to keep a general eye on the waterfront. Sometimes he would be at the pool, switching duties with Chuck, who was considered the lifeguard, but, for the most part, he spent his time on the dock. There was plenty of opportunity for Ellen Case to recognize him. He would see her through the corner of his eye as he walked around doing this and that. She looked at him frequently, but there was never a hint of recognition in her eyes. After a few days of waiting he knew she did not know who he was.

One afternoon he was down on the dock, doing

small jobs in the shack. He heard a girl's voice behind him, at the door. At the moment, he was putting new batteries into a flashlight.

"Will you bring me to my boat?"

He turned and saw Ellen. His face was expressionless.

"I'm Ellen Case," she said.

Tom stepped onto the dock and looked out at the water.

"Chuck has the speedboat out," he said.

They looked across the water and saw Chuck towing a water skier.

She smiled at him.

"I can row you out."

Getting into the rowboat, she said, "It's that one over there. The blue one-ten."

Tom dropped her at the boat, noticing how smoothly she went from one to the other, taking a giant step with her long bare legs. He stood off for a moment, watching. She was obviously a little flustered.

"Your halyard's fouled," he said.

She looked up and down the mast, shielding her eyes from the sun.

"What do you mean, my halyard's fouled?"

He came up to the one-ten again, getting on quickly, stepping to the foot of the mast in front of her, uncleating one end of the halyard and twisting it around itself until it ran free.

Then he took a step back, bumping into her. The cockpit was small and she had been standing close to him, watching what he was doing. He wrapped his arms around her and kissed her on the mouth. She wriggled and tried to hit him in the stomach with a small fist, but he pressed her against him, making any further efforts impossible. Suddenly she tightened and

109

stretched herself against him, leaning, gripping his shoulders.

He released her and gently kissed her on the lips, and then jumped lightly back into the rowboat, making the one-ten rock. She staggered against the boom and became quite red.

As he was rowing away, facing her, she said, softly, "You certainly don't waste time, do you?"

"Don't foul your halyards," he said.

At the dock, Chuck was waiting for him. He had tied up a few minutes before and had seen it all. He looked at Tom with slight disgust.

"Sucker," he said.

Tom dragged the rowboat onto the dock.

"All in good clean fun," he answered.

Ten

When Ellen Case came back from sailing she seemed in no hurry to leave the dock. She had not been gone long. Tom had looked up as he went about his duties on the dock, watching her across the water. The one-ten is a racing boat, and takes firm management. He noticed she was competent, but not brilliant. She was doing all the proper things at the proper times, but not smoothly. She sailed as if she were out of practice, or not completely familiar with the boat, or as if she knew she was being watched. She made the mooring well enough, coming around in a full arc, pulling up into the wind just below the mooring and shooting up to it. She was dead in the water just as she came abeam of the buoy. She did not have to try twice. Chuck was waiting for her in the speedboat. He brought her to the float, and went off to pick up someone else across the harbor.

Tom kept himself busy. He was not doing anything important, simply going over loose pieces of line, seeing what could be salvaged, cutting off frayed sections and splicing the two pieces. It could have been done anytime. He completely ignored her. She appeared to be waiting for whomever Chuck had gone to fetch. She looked over the water to see where the speedboat was. Then she knelt on the edge of the float and stared into the water looking at the swarms of Tommy Cods which poured out from under it. She sat, then, and upending her left foot toward her face, inspected it as if for a splinter. She did not operate. Tom was watching her out of the corner of his eyes. He was in the shack. She was very cute and moved like a child. She stood when she saw the boat coming in and waved. There was a lot of helloing as she grabbed the painter of the speedboat and made it fast to the ring. They were glad to see her, but she let them go up the ramp without her. Chuck followed grinning. She and Tom were left alone on the dock.

She put her head in the door of the shack.

"I suppose you know all the girls are in love with you," she said.

"I do," Tom answered. "Isn't it dreadful?"

She had come in and was leaning against the door frame, her hands behind her back.

"Are you terribly conceited?" she asked.

"Not a bit."

"I should think you would be. Everybody on Cape Cod knows who you are."

"Do they. Do they indeed." He smiled at the thought. "My name is Tom Mathews," he said.

It was hard to see her against the light.

She said, "I know."

She seemed disconcerted. He was being perfectly nice, smiling at her while they talked, glancing at her frequently. Still, he was busy with the line and not devoting himself to her. He knew what he had done in the boat was important to her; it was clear she thought it rather wonderful, in fact: a healthy, honest thing to do, although it had embarrassed her. Now his being so casual about it upset her a little.

"You must be awfully conceited," she said.

"Why?"

"Why else would you kiss me that way? Suppose I didn't want you to kiss me?"

"You did."

"Did I? How do you know."

"Didn't you?"

She guided her toe along a crack in the floor.

"Yes," she said. "But you had no reason to think so. Why did you kiss me?"

His look was perfectly frank. "Because you're sexy."

She colored.

"I don't mean to be."

"I know, but you are."

He knew he was confusing her. She turned to go.

"Don't go," he said.

"Why not, for heaven's sake?"

He chuckled. Asses and boobs, he thought.

"Because I like you."

She did a surprising thing, then. Tom was sitting on a stool, his bare knees apart, the line he was working on running over them. She came and stood between his knees, close to him, and put her hand on the side of his face, cupping it along his jaw bone. He put his head against her hand and touched his lips to her wrist. He was surprised at his own reaction to this simple act. There was a warm, delightful sensation at the back of his neck and through his head. He realized, with some feeling, that this was the first spontaneous thing he had ever done.

"You're very odd," she said. "I believe you truly feel something."

He swallowed.

"I do," he said.

"You do have feeling. The girls said you were a little cold."

He said nothing. He was not feeling cold.

They were gentle with each other. He put his hands on her hips and held her firmly. She had her hands over both his ears. He pressed his thumb against her hip bone and she wriggled and sat down on his knee. He kissed her.

He found the experience fantastic. His head swelled with good feeling. His stomach muscles tightened, his neck became straight, and his legs came together clamping her knees in a tight press. It was all automatic and natural. He had to pause for a moment.

She stood up and took a step to the door.

"See you later," she said gaily.

She went out and started up the ramp.

He followed her out of the shack.

"What time will I pick you up?"

"Seven-thirty," she said from the ramp. "Do you know my house?"

"I can find it," he answered.

She waved and went up the ramp.

Tom went back into the shack and sat down on the stool. He had never felt such a reaction. He was sure something was different about Ellen. Although Tom had had a variety of sexual experiences, he had never felt anything as strongly as that kiss. And it was all so innocent! He marveled at it. The girl must have extra magic. She certainly knew how to kiss and how to move and how to look at one. Was she being sincere? He did not know whether she had felt anything or not.

He wondered if he were sick. He felt his brow, finding it damp with sweat. He laughed at himself. Without doubt, he had been shaken by the experience. It must be that he had not been eating well. He and Chuck had been doing most of their eating from the Club snack bar, never having a full meal. He had been up late most nights.

He laughed again.

It had been a magnificent, warm, tender experience, and he had enjoyed it. But he could not figure what was the matter with him. He must eat better and sleep more. He could get over it.

That afternoon Tom lost Princeton.

Mister Perry had asked Tom to drive down to Morrison's Hardware to get some shackles. Tom was always glad to use his car in this way. It was only a half mile, and the ride in the convertible provided him with a chance to cool off. Since the hardware store was owned by Chuck's father, Tom waited until late in the afternoon to see if Chuck could go with him. Tom went up to the pool, saw there were still people around and noticed that Chuck was busy talking with three girls, so he did not bother to ask. Instead, he brought Princeton to heel and went through the gate to his car.

The top of the car was down and Princeton got into his usual position, standing with his hind legs on the front seat, his forepaws on the arm rest, his head out the window. Tom drove to the entrance to the road and stopped to let a car turn into the club driveway. The driver was the woman who owned the poodle bitch that Princeton had been trying to court. It was a big car with tail fins, and the woman drove it as if it were a battleship, taking the corner slowly and rolling forward at a crawl. Princeton lately had been flirting with the poodle bitch more than ever; but all his advances had been rebuffed. Even so, he had become more excited each time he saw her. Tom saw the poodle's face pressed against the back window of the car. She had seen Princeton. Tom hoped Princeton would not see her. She began to bark at Princeton from behind the closed window of the slowly moving car. Suddenly Princeton began to bark excitedly.

He leaped into the back seat and over the door frame into the street. There was another car just about to pass Tom on the left, coming toward him as Tom was pulling out of the driveway. There was a sharp squeal of brakes.

Tom stopped immediately and ran to where the other car had stopped. The man had gotten out and was looking helpless. Tom paid no attention to him. He ran around the car and saw Princeton crawling under a car which was parked on the other side of the road. Tom saw he was hurt, barely able to drag himself along. People were flooding out from the swimming pool. Roughly, he reached under the car and dragged the dog out, getting hold of his fur.

The dog was badly hurt. He was still alive but there was terror in his eyes. His left hind leg was joined to his body by only a piece of skin. His stomach had been torn open and come out, in a piece. His fur was drenched with blood.

Tom could not think how to kill him. He had left his knife on the float. He put his hands around Princeton's throat and held tight. It did no good. It was hard to exert real pressure through all the fur of the neck. He squeezed harder, using both hands, feeling the windpipe like a thin, rubbery cord between his fingers. Princeton was swallowing, putting his pink tongue through his tightly closed mouth, trying to breathe. Tom could feel something still going through the windpipe and he squeezed harder and harder. Princeton's head was turned at an angle away from him, looking aside, but he now and then glanced at Tom. There were both fear and patience in the eyes, as if he was being subjected to something he could not understand, but still trusted Tom. The boy held on, strangling his dog, squeezing more and more firmly. His arms and shoulders began to shake with the effort. He had had no idea a dog's neck could be so tough. Princeton's eyes glazed and his effort to swallow became less energetic. Sweat was pouring off Tom's brow and he closed his eyes. He felt Chuck come up beside him and make a feeble effort to make him stop. He continued squeezing the neck. Finally, he felt Chuck pounding him on the shoulder and he opened his eyes and saw that Princeton was dead. The body was limp in his hands. It had taken a dreadfully long time.

Tom sat back on the roadway, taking his fingers away from Princeton's neck. They were wet with blood and stiff from the effort and pieces of hair had stuck to them. They ached. He put them under his arm pits and waited for them to become less numb. He had never done anything so hard in his life. He was terribly tired. He stood up and, bending over again, picked Princeton up in his arms, bringing him to the car across the road. There was an old sailbag on the back seat and he put him in that. People were still watching him from across the road, standing in the sunlight in their shorts and swimming suits. He got into the car and drove off. Tom went to the hardware store to get the shackles. He said nothing about the accident to anybody, making his purchase quietly and easily, exchanging remarks with Mister Morrison. He counted out the price from the change in his pocket, using up three pennies he had rather than taking two pennies in change of a nickle or dime. He stopped and looked at some waterskis and asked Mister Morrison their price. He held the door open for a woman who was entering as he was leaving. He stopped at the newsstand to buy a *Boston Herald* and stood on the sidewalk taking a quick look at the sports pages. He acted as he would any other day.

Getting back into his car he drove out of the village and found a street running west. He knew he had a trench shovel in the trunk of his car, but he had to find someplace to bury Princeton. It was prudent of him to drive west, away from the sea. He knew the soil would be firmer away from the sand dunes and the marshes. He finally found a wooded place on an old dirt road, and, driving his car down a woodcutter's path, stopped at a little clearing. There was a brook there about a foot wide. Tom wondered if it might flood in spring, causing the surrounding soil to become soft. He took the sailbag from the back seat and the shovel from the trunk, going up a slight rise over the brook, putting the sailbag on the ground and digging a hole, about four feet deep, two feet by four feet. He had to lie on his stomach to get it deep enough. Then he put the sailbag in the hole and covered it up. He had been very methodical.

He scattered the extra dirt around in the woods and covered the grave with two or three inches of leaves and pine needles, making it look no different from the rest of the ground. No one would know anything had been buried there.

It was late when he got back to the Club. People had abandoned the pool, and Chuck had gotten dressed. He looked across the pool in a quizzical, uncertain way when Tom came through the arch, as if trying to assess how much strangling his dog had meant to Tom. He did not speak. Tom went through his shack, picked up his towel, and went to the shower area. He assumed Chuck was full of the usual questions and puzzlements. People did not see that sort of thing every day, and, when they did see it, they were apt to have an emotional reaction, although only bystanders. Tom knew this from experience, and although he was never sure exactly what that emotional reaction might be, he had no sympathy for it. It was a silly self-indulgence. Tom wished people would separate themselves from their emotions. It was all such a waste of energy and time.

Chuck came in while he was dressing. Tom was standing in front of his foggy, cracked mirror, working on his tie and whistling. Chuck lay down on the bed, propping himself up with one elbow.

He said, "I'm sorry, Tom."

"About what?" Tom stopped whistling.

"About Princeton. He was a nice dog. Almost human."

Better than human, Tom thought.

"I'm sorry you had to kill him that way."

"I wished I had had my knife," Tom said. "It would have been easier."

Chuck said, "He certainly was a mess."

Tom managed his tie and took a rag out of his chest of drawers and proceeded to dust his shoes, putting his foot on a wicker chair.

"The man who hit him talked to me after you left. He said he was awfully sorry but he couldn't stop in time. Apparently Princeton jumped out of your back seat into the roadway."

"He did," Tom said.

"He left his name and address. I told him you'd get in touch with him." He took his wallet and began rummaging for the piece of paper. "Do you want it?"

"No."

Chuck said, "Aren't you going to get in touch with him?"

"No."

"He felt awful sorry."

"I daresay."

"It wasn't his fault."

"I know. But what good would getting in touch with him do. He would say he was sorry and offer to buy me a new dog, even if his kids had to eat spaghetti all

119

week. He would just slobber all over me. To hell with it."

"All right," Chuck said. He put his wallet back. "Are you going out?"

"Yes."

"With who?"

"Ellen Case."

"Stupid."

"Why stupid?"

Tom was brushing his coat.

"They're not in your league."

"She's pretty nice," Tom said. "Good ass."

"I know, but she's not in your league. Mommy's got her cut out for a Harvard man who's going to be Secretary of State."

"Any Harvard man in particular?" Tom asked.

"Anyone that will become Secretary of State."

"Guess I'll have to become Secretary of State," Tom said.

"Not with the Case money, you won't."

Tom went to the door and opened it. He put his hand on the light switch but, before turning off the light, he turned to see if Chuck had anything more to say. Chuck had not moved from the bed.

Chuck said, "Tom, wait a minute."

"What?"

"I want to tell you something."

"Don't be shy about it."

"You strangled your dog this afternoon."

"I know that."

"I know it was the right thing to do. He really was a mess."

"So what."

"I just wanted to say I wouldn't have had the courage to do it."

Tom said, "I know that, too."

"I mean, it was something not everyone would do."

Tom snapped off the light. "Forget it. The bloody dog's dead."

Eleven

The door of the Case house was opened to Tom by a horsefaced woman. She smiled and looked ugly. The city servants Tom had known looked plain, by and large, but he had never seen one as ugly as this. He presumed she must be someone working for the Case family for the summer.

The woman asked Tom to go upstairs to the living room while she told Ellen he was here.

The inside of the house did not even try to keep up the Cape Cod pretense. It was about as quaint as the inside of a modern airliner. An open dining area was just inside the main door, backed by a wide, bright kitchen. Tom went up a stairwell to the right, and found himself at one end of a long, glass-walled living room. Against the inside wall was a huge fieldstone fireplace with a massive chimney. A few chairs and a sofa on a bright rug were facing the fireplace. On the other side of the fireplace was a walnut baby grand piano. Running along the inside wall, twelve feet off the floor, was a balcony which Tom presumed served as the upstairs hallway. It even ran behind the chimney. Closed, varnished doors were evenly spaced along the balcony. Thick, rough-hewn beams came down from the cathedral peak of the ceiling against the wall. The glass of the outside wall had sliding panels which led onto a deck over the beach. The sea was directly outside the windows. The living room was the core of the house and Tom gathered it was partly that cantilevered section he had seen from outside and had taken for a lounge.

At one end of the room were two alcoves. One evidently served as Case's workroom. In it there was a drawingboard, shelves for rolled blueprints, and a high chair. The room looked too neat to have had much use. But there was a drawing on the board. Tom looked at it, but could understand nothing of it except that it was a plan for this house. It seemed to have been left out for display purposes. The other alcove was a bar.

Tom turned back to the living room, looking at it from one end. The room must have been sixty feet long. There were paintings along the inside wall, under and over the balcony. They were uniformly abstracts, canvasses full of bright, swirling colors. He supposed they were worth quite a lot, but he knew little about non-objective art. He noticed none of the paintings had recognizable subjects, just lines and colors. There were no faces of people in the room. There was not so much as a magazine visible. There were no pipes, books, or other evidence that anyone had ever been there. The room was exquisite, and impersonal. It could have been the lobby of a business concern.

He heard Ellen's voice and looked up. She was standing above him on the balcony, her elbows on the railing.

"Hey, handsome, what are you looking at?" she had said.

"Your house," he answered. "I've never seen anything like it."

She skipped down the stairs.

"You should see the one in New Hope. My father's an architect."

123

"Where is he? I was hoping to meet him."

"They went to the Hodgson's for cocktails."

"Will it be all right if I take you out?"

"They don't care. They won't care beans."

In the car, she said, "Where are we going?"

"Well," he said. "We might have supper at the Pen and Pencil, see the new Lerner and Loewe, have a snack at Cerutti's, take a horse and buggy ride through the Park and spend the night at the Plaza. That all right?"

As always, with people, Tom began to play a role. He was acting.

"Is that what you'd do in New York?"

"Maybe. Or then again we might have a hamburg at Phoebe's, a flick at 72nd Street, a coke and a subway home."

"That sounds better."

"Or we could sit here and neck."

"Not here," she said. "We'd be in Mother's and Dad's way when they come in. They'd drive right through us. A few drinks make Dad convinced he's right."

"What do a few drinks do to your mother?"

"Make her convinced he's wrong."

"Poor fellow. Marriage is a rotten institution."

"Isn't it. But infidelity is worse. That way you never know whom you're fighting."

"How about a movie at the local palace?"

"What's playing?" she asked.

"Let me see. I think it's something about a horse. It's all about a cowboy what loves his horse and hates people. That all right?"

"What's the co-feature?" she asked.

"Oh, that. Well, that's a true to life depiction of the younger generation what rides around on motorcycles eating dill pickles and revolting the populace."

"Sounds good. Let's go."

"Or we could stay here and neck."

"That comes later," she said. "After the dill pickles and the horse."

The movie was not quite as Tom had described it. They had both forgotten the character of westerns had changed perceptibly in recent years, but they remembered it after they sat down in the theatre. Tom said this was one of the adult westerns, and she said she thought the kids would like that. Before the lights dimmed they spoke of the new type of cowboy being put out by Hollywood. Tom pointed out that the cowboy no longer cared for his horse, riding a different one each time he was chased. She agreed, saying he would hire it for a silver dollar at the town stable and never seem to return it. They clucked their tongues at the infidelity of the modern cowboy and then kept quiet while the film was on.

After the movie they drove out to the beach. She sat close to him and held his hand.

On the way, she said, 'You certainly ate an awful lot of popcorn."

"That's because I was so nervous."

"Were you afraid the bad man might get away?"

"No. I was afraid he might not."

He stopped the car at the beach and turned off the headlights. They could see and hear the waves breaking, white lines extending slowly up the beach.

"Where's the moon?" she asked. "I never spoon unless there's a moon to spoon to."

She lay on her back, putting her head on his lap.

He looked up, searching the sky. The top of the convertible was down. "There ain't no moon. No moon at all."

"Then I shan't spoon."

He tried to put his head down to kiss her face but

hit his forehead against the wheel, making the horn go off.

"You make it damned difficult," he said.

"Do you always sound that way when you're horny?" she asked.

"Very funny."

He put his hands under her shoulder blades and lifted her up. Her mouth was open, and she bit his nose.

"My God," he said, rubbing it. "You're a blinking riot."

Her head was in his lap again and she was laughing.

"No moon, no spoon," she said.

In one movement he put both hands under her body and sat her in his lap, kissing her. She tightened and banged him on the shoulder, enjoying it, and slowly he pressed sideways until he fell on top of her. Her head was on the seat near the other door. Both of their bodies were tight and moving. Never in his life had Tom done anything as innocent or as moving. Every inch of his skin felt tight and alive, every muscle taut. Force poured out of him and eagerness controlled him. He wanted to do so much more immediately, and he knew he could. She would agree, without question. He always knew his counterpart, and he had never guessed wrong. However, he restrained himself. He did not want that, not with her. He had an inkling there might be something more to this relationship, something deeper, more wonderful: something he had never seen or felt or known. She might be able to show him. He did not want to risk disappointing her, in herself. He could not have her give him everything, if it were her first time. He was sure she was a virgin and knew that no matter what he did, she would feel disappointed in herself the first time, especially facing his eagerness.

The danger was she could then go home to mother. It would take her days or weeks to get over the resentment, if she ever did, and he would not be able to get at her. He was calculating all these things while they kissed. He was being far more restrained than she knew.

As it was, they were going through the regular routine of necking in a car. Lying on top of her, he kissed her on the mouth, one hand under her head, the other under her jaw. He kissed her again, with greater passion, hunching his shoulders to bring full weight against her mouth. Then he began, slowly to move his hips. He felt her hands tear his shirt free from his belt and slide up the bare skin of his back, pulling him down to her even closer. Then her hips began to move with his. Her jaw was up, forcing her mouth as hard as possible against his. They were both breathing hard through their noses, and occasionally she would gulp air. He began to rub his leg against her, bringing his knee up as far as her hip and down again to her knee. All this was the routine way of doing things, for both of them. But this was the first time he had felt so much. He wanted to have her. But he knew it would be a mistake. Even though she would give herself to him, he was sure, her resentment at having lost her virginity on her first date with him, in a car, at the beach, could never be overcome. He restricted himself to the doing of these usual things.

"My golly, Charlie," she said. "You want to grind me through the seat?"

"It's always fun trying," he said.

"Wow."

He eased much of his weight off her.

"Do you always carry on like that?" she asked.

"No," he said. He had never felt quite that way before. "Only when there is no moon."

127

"I see a moon," she said.

He craned his neck and looked up.

"There's no moon."

"I see a moon."

"All right. You see a moon. Is it made of green cheese?"

"No. It's made of ah, let me see, uh, tin foil."

"Oh, well then. That's all right."

He kissed her again.

"There's that damn moon again," she said.

He was gentle with her then. He loved the feeling of her hair. It was soft and fluffy and smelled wonderful. She was clean and lovely and happy. She was making Tom feel something and they both knew it. She seemed delighted with herself.

"You're the best kisser in all the world," she said.

"That's cause I practice."

"Do you? Everyday?"

"Every damn day. I got callouses."

"It's worth it. Let me practice with you?"

"You've got to have a card," he said. "Do you belong to the Union?"

"What Union?"

"The American Affiliated Kissers. The AAK."

"No, but I would like to belong to the AAK, sir. Might I belong to the AAK? Can you arrange it?"

"We'll see."

"Aren't I good enough?"

"Oh, your work is all right. It's who you know that counts. Whom do you know?"

"Well, let me see. I know my mother and I know my father and I know—I used to know . . ."

She moved her body, indicating she wanted to get up. He let her up. They sat in the still, dark car side by side.

All her happiness was gone, as if deflated by the

prick of a thought. She was silent a moment, allowing her fingers to pick at each other in her lap.

"Is it like this with you, with all the other girls?"

"No."

"I believe it. They said you were fine, but cold. I did not get that feeling."

"They said that?"

"Of course," she smiled. "What do you think."

"Why, those dirty rats. See if I ever buy them popcorn again."

She took his hand. "I like you."

"Will you report well of me?"

"Very well. I'll say, 'That Tom Mathews. What a kisser!'"

"That's good."

"But then the other girls will think I'm odd, too. I'd better say nothing. I'll just go around looking superior and smug. That will show them."

"Indeed it will."

She put her head against his shoulder again.

"I'm glad you asked me out, Tom. Of course the pickings are slim. Most of the girls are away somewhere. And you've gone through the rest of them before I even arrived."

"Why are you here this summer?"

She did not answer.

He continued. "Chuck said you normally spend very little time here in the summer."

Her voice was quiet. "My brother died this spring, in April. I thought I could help my parents through it if I stayed home, this summer."

He said nothing.

"I don't seem to be helping much," she said. "The only difference it makes is that my mother cries now when she gets drunk and my father becomes quiet."

"What do they do when they're not drunk?"

"Drink."

"All because of your brother?"

"No, they always drank. Everybody drinks, haven't you noticed? No, the only difference is that now when they drink she cries and he gets quiet."

"Stop feeling sorry for yourself."

"I'm not feeling sorry for myself. I don't care about them. They're just like everybody else's parents. They fly all the way to the goddamned Riviera to drink the same old stuff they could get at home. My brother committed suicide."

Tom held tightly onto her hand, wanting to support her, help her through what she was saying.

"He was a year older than I am, just nineteen. He played a mean trumpet and was doing well at school. He was a good looking guy, too, I guess, although not as good looking as you are."

"What do you suppose made him do it?" Tom asked. He began feeling something in his left eye and rubbed it with the fingers of his left hand, turning his head away from her.

"Mac was a little high strung."

It seemed odd to Tom to have Casey called Mac. It had never occurred to him that Casey might have a different name. Of course the family would not call him Casey. Funny he had never realized it.

"A girl?" he asked.

She did not answer right away.

"Is that why boys usually commit suicide?"

"I guess so. I don't know."

Tom was keeping his head averted, looking at the beach through the left hand side of the windshield.

"He had a roommate who was very handsome. His name was Tom Betancourt." She paused after saying the name, as if the sound of it sickened her. "They had been roommates all through prep school and college.

130

Mac killed himself on a Sunday afternoon while the other boy, Betancourt, watched."

"Were they drunk?"

He was surprised to hear himself ask the question. It was as if he were being swept along in a conversation as a third person, genuinely unacquainted with what he was being told.

"No," she said. "They weren't drunk. Why do you suppose he would do it?"

"I don't know," Tom said. "I wish I did."

"It was really awful."

"Ellen, you said your brother's roommate was handsome. Why did you say that?"

"That was all Mac ever said about him. He lives in New York, and his father is a lawyer. I never met him."

Tom was wondering. An idea was beginning to build in his mind, but he could not quite reach it.

"Now I'm all depressed," she said. "And I was so happy."

"Cheer up," he said, starting the car. "We all have suicides happen to us, and not knowing why is just part of it."

Driving back to her house, he asked her to go to a beach party with him the next night.

"Will it help me get into the Union?"

"It might help."

"All right, then. I'll come."

Tom left her at her house, without going in. She had told him of a short cut back to the Club, a secondary road that ran along the shore. Tom drove it, being very careful. It was less than secondary. For the most part it went through the marshes, winding in and out. There was barely room for two cars to pass. There were no lights at all along the road, and it was posted throughout for twenty-five miles per hour. At one point there

131

was a long, low cement bridge carrying the road over a particularly hopeless marsh. It had been built during the depression when the government had needed to put men to work. Coming off that bridge there was a dangerous and unexpected turn back into the marshes. Tom knew he would have to remember that. He was a very careful driver and was always able to remember things of that sort. He took pride in never making a mistake.

Twelve

Strangling Princeton apparently did not bother Tom in the slightest. The people coming to the Club the next day were grieved to hear Princeton had been killed, especially in such an ugly way. The story got around rapidly.

No one could understand Tom's reaction. He came and went by himself, saying hello to people, stopping to speak if someone spoke to him, smiling and laughing at a joke. There was nothing sad or downhearted about him at all. A few people said he was making a good show of it, but even these looked into his eyes and could find nothing there. They thought him very odd. Surely he had been attached to the dog; he must have been, in order to have the patience to do all that training. How could he not love Princeton? They gave Tom that look of puzzlement Tom had seen often before. He thought nothing of it. If they expected him to react emotionally over the death of a dog, they were silly. It was their weakness, not his. By early afternoon they had adjusted to the fact that Tom was not going to react to the loss of his dog and the looks of puzzlement abated.

When both Tom and Chuck were free that afternoon. Tom suggested water skiing, and Chuck agreed. The speedboat was not being used for anything else. They went down to the float, and Tom sat on its edge, his feet and the skis dangling in the water. He had taken the line and when Chuck swung the boat out the slack was taken up quickly; Tom's skis surfaced easily and beautifully. They went across the harbor in no time and then began to go around and about, back and forth.

Water skiing is not a difficult sport, if it is a sport at all and not merely a sensation, and not very hazardous. For some reason or other, however, Tom insisted on making it hazardous. The boat was a heavy, inboard speedboat and Chuck drove at almost top speed, never hesitating to turn quickly or swerve. Tom would head directly for a nun, can, or other buoy, passing it with only inches to spare. More than once he had found red or black paint along the edges of his skis when he got in. He would calculate the drift of mooring lines and go over them at such a point that if he veered two inches to the left or right his ski would catch and trip him. But he never did smash into a buoy or catch his ski. He simply came as close as he could without having an accident. He was not being careless; quite the contrary. He was extraordinarily careful. He could not do such things without having accidents unless he had been careful. Tom had never had an accident.

When he returned to the dock, Ellen Case was storming down the ramp. She had been watching from the porch of the Club house and had started down when she saw him coming in. Her face was white and the skin around her eyes tight. Her hands were in fists. She was furious.

She marched up to where he sat on the edge of the dock, taking off his skis.

"Tom Mathews," she said, fists on her hips. "Don't you ever do that again."

He stood up. "Do what?"

"Don't you ever ski like that again! You frightened

134

me half to death. Don't you ever do anything like that again! Ever ever ever!"

"What on earth are you talking about?"

Whereupon she swung and hit him, square on the cheekbone. His feet were wet and the dock was wet from his dripping swimsuit, which put him a little off balance. He fell down, landing in a sitting position. He had not been expecting it.

"Don't you ever do that!" she said.

She stamped up the ramp towards the Club. Tom was stunned. Such a thing had never happened to him before. He had never been hit in anger, especially by a female, and he certainly had never been knocked down. For the life of him, he could think of no good reason for her to do that.

He followed her up the ramp, calling her. She paid no attention, walking faster. He did not catch her until she was in the parking lot starting her car. He rushed out to stop her from driving off, even though the hot gravel hurt his bare feet.

He leaned on the car door to take some of his weight off his burning feet. His hands were on the hot metal of the window sill.

"Why did you do that?" he asked.

"Because you were being stupid. Stupid and foolish and careless. Showing off. You could have hurt yourself."

"But I didn't."

"Get out of my way."

"Are you trying to take responsibility for me?" The question blurted out.

"Yes, goddamn it, I am."

She drove off, though Tom was still leaning against the car.

He jumped back and scratched his head, watching her go around the corner into the roadway. It was the most peculiar behavior he had ever seen. For some reason she had become enraged to see him water skiing; enraged and possibly frightened. What difference should it make to her if he got hurt?

Showing off: the words nettled him. Nothing was farther from his thoughts. Certainly he did not care what anybody thought. Water skiing was a sport and, as with any other sport, Tom felt it should be honed to a fine edge of performance. One could not know if one was perfect in performance until one pushed one's ability to the point where any imperfection would become apparent. If one did not water ski well enough, one deserved to be smashed into a buoy. Tom was hot with anger. He had never been spoken to like that.

He walked gingerly over the gravel toward the pool. He was trying to understand why Ellen Case thought she had the right to take responsibility for him. Suddenly the heat of his anger turned to a warm glow. He comprehended. She loved him. She did not want to see him get hurt, simply because she cared for him. His water skiing had frightened her. He smiled at himself. This was the first time in his experience he realized, anyone had felt that way towards him. In prep school, his housemother would scold him for going out on a wet day without his rubbers: but her scoldings had been empty and professional. No one had ever slugged him for not taking care of himself. He laughed out loud. In loving him Ellen Case did give herself the right to take some responsibility for him.

Going through the pool area, still grinning to himself, he heard a "yoo hoo" and turned to see a woman sitting in a chaise longue sunning herself and beckoning to him. She was smiling sweetly. He had never seen her before.

He went over to her.

"You're Tom Mathews, aren't you?"

She had a kerchief wrapped around her hair and was wearing sunglasses.

"Yes, Ma'm."

"I'm Mrs. Case, Ellen's mother. Would you like a drink?"

She had a highball.

"No, thank you."

"Sit down anyway. I want to talk to you."

Tom could see her eyes behind the sunglasses. She probably wore them on purpose, feeling that her eyes could not be seen. They were drinking him in, looking at his stomach and at his shoulders and at whatever else interested her. Tom looked down. Just above his swimming trunks his stomach was wet with sweat and gleaming in the sun. When he looked back at her, she was looking into his eyes.

He sat down in a chair turned at a slight angle to her.

"Ellen tells me you took her out last night. Was it fun?"

"Yes, Ma'm."

"I think she likes you, Tom. By the way, do you know you have a welt on your cheekbone?"

"Yes, Ma'm."

Tom did not put his hand up.

"I'm afraid it's bleeding," she said, as if urging him to do something about it.

Tom still did not put his hand up to investigate his bruise.

"It's not your eye, is it?" she asked.

"No, Ma'm."

"Well, that's good. We definitely have that established. You are bleeding from your cheekbone, but your eye is all right."

She began to look at Tom as if she thought him very odd indeed.

"They tell me your dog died yesterday, Tom."

"Yes, Ma'm. He did."

She ran her eyes over his shoulders again, and down his arms.

"I'm terribly sorry. I like dogs, too. Was he a very old dog?"

"No, Ma'm."

"He wasn't a very old dog."

"No."

"Then it's especially too bad."

"Yes, Ma'm."

She shifted her position in the chaise longue. Tom knew he was making her a little uncomfortable.

She said suddenly, almost incredulously, "Ellen says you're very bright." It was clear she could not understand how anybody could say Tom was very bright.

"I am," he said.

"Good. Then we have three things definitely established. Although your face is bleeding, your eye is all right; it's too bad your dog is dead because he was not very old; and you are bright. It's always good to know the boys Ellen is dating. Are you sure you wouldn't like a drink?"

"No, thank you."

"May I ask why you wouldn't like a drink?"

He thought for a moment, squinting into the sun. He had his hands under his thighs. He said, "Because continual, daily drinking is accumulative, fattening, weakening, and a bore."

He had continued looking at the sky as he spoke.

"My," she said, "but we are getting a lot of things established."

"I do drink," he said, looking at her. "Occasionally."

"And do you neck passionately?"

He rocked forward on his hands, resettling his legs. "Yes, Ma'm."

She stopped asking questions for a moment. Her hand was under her chin and she was looking at Tom openly.

A fat, blotchy-looking man came up with a drink in his hand and sat down in a deck chair the other side of the chaise longue. He was wearing damp, green swimming trunks. There was a bright, striped beach towel on the chair and he had sat upon it.

Mrs. Case was still looking at Tom.

"This is Mister Case," she said, not looking at him. "Tom Mathews, the young man Ellen's been dating."

Tom began to rise but Case motioned him down. He flopped his hand at Tom as if to say the introduction was not worth their rising. Tom returned to his original position.

"So far," Mrs. Case said, "this odd savage and I have established that although he is bleeding from the face there is nothing wrong with his eye; that his dog was not old, but he died; that he is very bright indeed; that he does not like to drink because it's fattening; and that he necks passionately."

Case looked at Tom uncertainly, but did not speak to him. He took a drink and put his glass on the flagstones at his feet.

"What does your father do, Tom?" Mrs. Case asked.

"He's a lawyer, Ma'm. In New York."

"Oh? What firm is he with?"

Tom wanted to appear to be lying. "Mathews and Smith," he said. He knew she would take it as a pretension. He was right.

"How nice," she said, smiling. "And what will you do when you grow up?"

"I thought I might be an architect."

Tom wanted to get a rise out of Case. But there was no response. Case could not even pretend interest in this young man of Ellen's.

Mrs. Case put down her glass. "Tom's perfectly right," she said. "We must change our ways. Let's all have a lemonade. Tom, would you get me a lemonade?"

"Of course."

In order to get to the snack bar from the pool he had to go along a high cement wall facing the sea and stand at the counter a few minutes. Coming back along the wall with the cup of lemonade in his hand, he ran into Mrs. Case.

She greeted him by putting her hands up to his neck, fondling his ears.

"You took so long," she said.

Tom was standing still, his bare feet on the hot walk. He could feel the reflection of the heat from the cement wall against his bare back. He was holding the cup of lemonade between them in one hand. He was looking into the cup, thinking.

"You really are a handsome boy," she said.

She ran her hands down his neck and out the length of his shoulders.

Tom sighed.

She took a step towards him, moving around the cup of lemonade with her hips, leaving that hand behind her. Tom's other hand was at his side. He was still looking down, wishing all this were not happening. He was afraid his efforts to know the Case family would be short-lived. Ellen need never know about this. Mrs. Case continued to move in on him, slowly.

Hunching her shoulders forward, she put her breasts against his ribs and then stood up on her toes. The top of her bathing suit rolled down as she pressed in and up. Tom's eyes were still down. Her breasts were bare against his chest.

He put his other arm around her and kissed her hard on the mouth, shoving his tongue through her teeth. At the same time, with his right hand, he poured the cold lemonade down her back. As she tried to jump away from him, he held her tight with his arms and rubbed the lemonade over her back with his free hand. He dropped the paper cup then, and rubbed with both hands, going under her bathing suit, smoothing the lemonade all over her posterior.

He then released her, and she staggered against the wall. In the sunlight her eyes were green with shock and hatred.

Tom said, "Tell your daughter I'll pick her up at seven-thirty, will you?"

He walked to the edge of the swimming pool, dove in, swam across it under water, and popped out the other side. He walked through the arch towards the float.

Thirteen

Tom picked Ellen up at her house that night.

"Oh, you poor dear," she said. "I'm so sorry I slugged you."

Tom grinned. There was a large, blue welt just below his right eye.

"Left hand, too," he said.

She kissed him, gently. "I promise I'll never slug you again. Forgive me?"

"I don't care. Slug me all you want."

In the car, driving out the long, sandy road, he said, "Your parents aren't at home tonight, either."

"No, they went over to Talmudsens' for cocktails. They only came in to dress. My mother said she met you."

"She did meet me."

"Isn't she awful?" asked Ellen.

"What did she say about me."

"I told you you were conceited. You want to hear good things about yourself."

"Did she say any good things?"

"She said you were so handsome you almost look weird."

Tom snorted.

"And she said she thought you were rather dumb."

"Wonder where she got that idea."

"She said all you said was yes ma'm and no ma'm and told her nothing. And she said, besides being dumb, you were poor and had no prospects. Then she said anyone who married you would be in trouble."

"Why in trouble?"

"Because you're too good looking. Manly and all that, but just too damned handsome. She said any girl would have trouble holding onto you. Women would be all over you."

"Did anybody ask either of you to marry me?"

"No, but the answer is yes, for both of us. Only you wouldn't like being married to her."

"No. I wouldn't."

"She's made Pop a drunk, and she's a drunk herself."

"Why?"

"Because everybody else is. Anyone who doesn't drink is very lonely, she says. Mmm, I love you. Let's stop talking about the bears and the beasts."

"All right. Got your towel?"

"Yup."

"And your weiners?"

"Yup."

"And your sun lotion?"

"The sun isn't out."

"I forgot."

"The moon is, though. Isn't that lovely?"

"That's not the moon. That's tin foil."

"That's a very good-looking hunk of tin foil, then. It's funny the way the tin foil comes up before the sun goes down."

"It's a ham."

"What?"

"It's a ham."

"Oh."

There were a lot of people on the beach when they

143

got there, all of them young. They had spread out a few blankets, and the boys were dragging wood to make a fire. Beer was in plaid tin boxes and the cans always blew up as they were opened. Most of the plaid tin boxes had spent part of the day in the trunks of hot cars.

Ellen was wearing white shorts with a red shirt, white sneakers and socks. It was a convenient costume, brief, neat, and cool. They strolled across the sand, hand in hand, to the camp fire, and plopped down on their knees. The last rays of the sun, mingled with the flicker of the beach fire, lighted her tanned face into red, yellow, and brown. The red shirt cast a dusky hue over her throat. She was alluring to say the least. For all that, she might have been in an apron and gingham dress. She was used to being the way she was that night. Sand and sea and bare skin were natural to her. She was smiling slightly, kneeling in the sand, leaning on her hands, her arms straight. She was returning his look evenly.

Chuck gave them each a beer and Tom asked if they needed help collecting wood. He was told to sit still. Chuck had seen the exchange of looks between the two.

Tom was wearing a blue button-down shirt, khaki slacks over his bathing trunks, loafers and white socks. It was regulation. He sat facing Ellen, an edge of the fire between them, his knees up, heels into the sand, beer can in hand.

Their eyes met and held each other for a long time. The flickering fire light between them caused a strain on their eyes. At first, they were intensely aware they were looking at each other. Then Tom began to think about Ellen Case. His look became even more intense, and he could feel the joy going out of his eyes. He was sure now she loved him; it was in her look; and this gave her certain rights to him. He was afraid of what that might mean. He had never allowed anyone into him before. And the times people had entered, whether he had wanted them to or not, there had just been hurt as a result. He was afraid of that hurt. He was saddened by the thought that it had become his nature not to let anyone love him. He wanted Ellen Case to love him. But he was afraid he would not let her. He was confused. He knew he was looking at her sadly, and without explanation. He could not help himself.

She came to him, crawling on her knees about the edge of the fire, and put her head in his lap.

"Oh, Tom," she said. "Don't be so serious."

He stood up abruptly and walked down the beach. He stood by the water edge, quietly a moment, looking at the reflection of the moonlight in the bay. Then he picked up a few stones and skipped them over the surface of the moonlit water.

She came down to him.

"Come on," he said. "Let's go for a swim."

He kicked his shoes up the beach and threw his shirt and trousers after them.

"I haven't a suit on under this."

He examined her shorts and shirt.

"They won't sink you."

"I know."

"Or you could take them off."

He turned his head towards the sea. His heart was beating rapidly. The fact that he was not acting with her made him almost restless. He had dropped his role. He was expressing a real want to her.

"All right," she said. "But you keep yours on."

"I will."

She took off the sneakers and socks, flinging them up the beach, and they ran along the water's edge, holding hands. The waves came up and washed their legs. He broke away from her and began to splash her, cupping his hand and scooping the water up. She ran to the edge of the water, following a wave, but before she was entirely out he had tackled her, making her fall headlong into the sand. They were rolling and laughing, and with her help he stripped her and she wriggled away and darted into the water. He dove in after her and swam under her until he reached her ankles and, pulling on her legs made her fall down. She had been standing, looking for him. Under the water she kicked at him and swam away from him, and he kept trying to catch her, his hands running down the length of her body. They would laugh at each other and swallow water and cough and gulp and immediately be submerged again. They were playing in the water with all the innocence of young children and neither of them had ever been so happy and excited. They were young; they were free; they were beautiful; they were in no danger from each other; they felt all the excitement of seven-year-olds at play combined with the wonderful suspense and passion of their own youth. They got quite out of breath.

"Hold everything!" she said.

"I'm trying to."

They fell into the water again and rolled around, laughing and gulping water. They became dizzy, and they were gasping for air. She stood up and walked away towards shore so that her breasts and stomach and thighs were out of water. She paused a moment, breathing hard. She was in a perfect pose. The moonlight was on her skin, making her tanned shoulders look rich and milky, and her breasts were as white as anything he had ever seen. He swam up to her and sat in the water, crossing his legs around her feet. Looking up, he could see her long legs glistening from the sea water and her breasts standing out above her hips.

"I've got to get my breath," she said.

"All right. Hurry up."

"I am hurrying."

"Time's up."

He dumped her into the water and held her head down and ducked under himself and kissed her. It seemed so outrageously simple and innocent they both laughed and she stepped on his stomach, making him swallow water. He came up coughing, and stood up. She stood in front of him, splashing him, and finally came into his arms. Her body was long and clean and completely firm. He thought he would not be able to stand it. The tension and suspense of that moment, when both of their bodies were drawn taut and pressed against each other, kissing, was the most magnificent he had ever felt. The gentleness of the kiss surprised them both.

"Oh my God," he said.

"You promised."

"I'll stick to it. I don't know why, but I'll stick to it."

He pressed his nose against her cheek and saw the moonlight sparkling in her wet skin.

"My God, you're lovely."

"I love your stomach," she said. Her hand was on it, her thumb kneading his navel. "It's nice and flat and hard and it is solid muscle. Where do you put your food, Tom?"

"Same place you put yours."

"I'm not so hard."

"Let me see. Where do I put my food. I keep it in my cheeks like a kangaroo and only swallow upon the special request of a corpuscle."

"Do kangaroos do that?"

"No. But they ought to. I mean, it's not their fault they don't."

"You know, you have a belly button I've been admiring for days."

"I have?"

"Yes. It's flat against your stomach rather than folded over or facing downward. You hardly ever see them that way."

"My, my."

"You can look it straight in the eye. It's a good, honest belly button. You hardly ever come across a good, honest belly button."

They went up to the beach and she lay on her back. The moonlight on her body made her the color of sand, but Tom touched the smoothness of her.

"Don't you do anything," she said.

"I won't. I would, but I won't."

"What does that mean?"

"Any other girl."

"You feel towards me as you would your sister?"

She touched him and knew it was not so.

"No, I feel something else."

"Like what?"

"Like love. I won't do anything you don't want. It might kill me, but I won't."

"It's not that I don't want, Tom. You know that."

"I know. We're thinking the same thing."

"It doesn't have to be marriage. I've made up my mind about that. But it shouldn't be too quick or too soon. There ought to be something permanent to it, at least the first time."

"I know."

"Anyway, I want to get my union card first. American Federation of Smoochers. A.F. of S."

His head was on her stomach, then, listening to her heart beat. It was as rapid as a rabbit's.

"You have great breasts," he said.

"Great big breasts?"

148

"No. Just great breasts."

"That's honest admiration."

"And you have great legs and great hips."

"I do wish you'd use another word."

"You're great."

"Gargantuan."

"You're trim and slim and skinny and smooth."

"Great. When do I get my card?"

"Anytime now. Forthcoming."

They were very gentle with each other, loving each other as if they were precious and liable to tear. They both knew it would not take much to place them beyond the bounds of restraint, and, for whatever reasons, good or foolish, neither wanted that, just yet. They were young and healthy and there was no war on and there were lots of tomorrows that needed looking forward to. They wanted each other, badly, and it was apparent in the beat of their hearts and the movements of their limbs, in their inhale and exhale. But they wanted the thought of tomorrow more, the continued anticipation, hope, tension, and suspense. The thinking was all very reasonable to Tom, and he went along with it, hard as it was. He had had enough experience in these matters to know it was true. Better than she, he was able to react to the reason of desire as being desirable, rather than satisfaction. At the same time there was a feeling entirely new to him. He did not want to hurt her or disappoint her or have her spend herself too quickly and not be satisfied with herself. Hurting her in any way would have horrified him. He had realized it that afternoon when she had knocked him down. She had been frightened he might be hurt. She was angry at him for taking useless chances. She cared for him, and he would not hurt her for anything in the world.

In a while, they started back to the beach party. They had difficulty finding her shorts, but found them

149

safe and dry. Tom's shoes and shirt were soaked; they never did find his trousers or socks. They must have gone with the tide. Everyone at the fire was singing and roasting marshmallows and drinking beer.

"Hi-ho!" yelled Chuck.

He was convinced he was drunk again.

"Where you cotton pickers been? Out pickin cotton?"

The two of them smiled quietly and sat down by the fire together and took up marshmallow sticks. Someone handed Tom a beer, and they shared it, drinking out of the can. People were trying to sing a song, but the effort failed each time. *In the Evening by the Moonlight* would be started doggedly only to run headlong into *Harvest Moon*. What the singing needed was an organizer, someone who would run around clapping his hands and shouting instructions as to when what parts were to sing and to ruin the whole thing. There was no organizer and they all had a splendid time, singing their different songs, together.

Chuck came over and nudged Tom, giving him an affected drunken wink. Asses and boobs, Tom thought. Asses and boobs.

"Are you all right, Tom?"

"I'm fine, Chuck."

"You two were up the beach for quite a while."

"Were we?"

"I mean, she didn't corrupt you, did she."

He thought he was being hilarious.

"She tried."

Chuck stood up.

"Everybody! Be quiet!" He waved his arms in the air. No one was being quiet. "I want you to meet the next Secretary of State!"

Then he fell down and laughed.

Ellen said, "What's all that about?"

150

"Chuck's had his heart on you for quite a while, I guess. He figures you're too rich for him."

"Oh."

"He thinks you have to marry the future Secretary of State, whoever he may be."

"I do. You don't think I'm bothering with you for nothing, do you?"

"Of course not."

"You're head of the A. F. of S. now. That's a pretty good start."

He was leaning against a sand dune looking into the fire, and she put her head in his lap.

"Are you going to tell Chuck what great breasts I have?"

"Boobs."

"What?"

"Boobs. He calls them boobs."

"Oh. Are you going to tell him?"

"Sure. I'm going to tell him everything. You females talk a lot."

"We sure do."

"Your mother says I'm dumb and weird."

"She's just jealous."

"I know."

"Are you going to tell him?"

"No."

"That's good. I want everything to be just between us. You and me. I want the sun to be a secret and the flowers to be a secret and the tin foil to be a secret."

"The tin foil will certainly be a secret."

"Just between you and me," she murmured. "Just between you and me."

For the rest of the beach party they sat silently, gazing into the fire. Once or twice, when he looked down at her head in his lap, he could see the brightness of the fire reflected in her eyes. He knew she was thinking, and he guessed, about him. He did not disturb her. He smoothed her hair with his hand.

They left the party a little after twelve. There was still a group of singers around the fire.

Getting into the car, she said, "I've decided I have you all figured out. Is that news?"

He was putting his wet loafers on the floor of the car. He would have to drive barefooted.

"No," he said.

"Well, I have. I have you all figured out, Tom Mathews."

He smiled to himself at hearing the name. It was not a happy smile. He was starting the car.

"Would you like to hear about it?"

Backing the car around, he said, "Sure."

"Well," she said. "I figure it's all because you're so sensitive. You're painfully sensitive, in the truest sense of the words. You feel so much and so deeply, you're afraid to feel at all. You find it very difficult to love, because you know that love can hurt. Another person can take this love, and take the hurt that goes along with it. But you're so sensitive you think such hurt would kill you. You needed to love Princeton, but you couldn't. You knew he was a dog, and someday he would die. You knew that if you loved him you wouldn't be able to stand that. You wouldn't be able to stand even the death of a dog you loved. So you didn't love him at all. A couple of days ago you were able to strangle him to death. A brave and noble thing to do. But you could do it because you had no feeling for the dog whatsoever."

They were driving down the winding road towards her house. He slumped over the wheel.

He said nothing.

"You're like a little kid who locks himself in his room," she continued, "because he knows the next person he sees will make him have a temper tantrum. You won't involve yourself with people because you know if you ever got really involved you'd go out of control. You've got so much feeling that if you ever allowed yourself to feel you'd go wild. Therefore you don't let yourself feel at all. You've tied yourself up in a nice tight little package of self-protection. You know you're perfectly safe as long as you feel nothing."

He turned into her driveway.

"Everyone else thinks you're cold and aloof and inhuman," she said. "Especially since you strangled Princeton. I don't. I think you're probably more sensitive than anyone in the world."

All the way home he had said nothing, in either agreement or disagreement. He had just been listening, closely.

Before she got out of the car, she took his face in her hand and turned it toward her, to kiss him. She saw that his cheeks were wet and she could feel the tears on his skin beneath her fingers.

She looked at him a moment. He was not trying to hide his face.

"You see," she said. "I was right."

She kissed him gently on the mouth and jumped out of the car.

Leaving her, then, driving away from her house, Tom was happier than he had ever been.

Fourteen

Tom Betancourt was in love.

The night of the beach party, after he brought Ellen Case home, he drove around for hours, chuckling to himself and feeling rather silly. The top was still down on the car and the night was warm and he was exhilarated. He drove over all the roads of the Cape, finding himself in Hyannisport and Orleans and finally Wellfleet before turning back. The radio was on, playing the popular music loudly, and he sang to each song, knowing neither the words nor the music but being convinced, all the same, that he was the greatest hidden talent since Harry Belafonte was a boy. The air was clean and salty. The large old houses he had passed were silent, sitting in their yards of big trees and little lawns. He drove fast and he drove slowly. Anyone seeing him would have thought him drunk.

He was elated. Even though it was almost dawn when he got back to the Club and fell on his bed, he could not sleep. Ellen Case was lovely: she was beautiful, and warm, and tender; she understood; she was good, and cautious, and sensible; she was loving, and kind, and generous. He could not understand himself. Why had he never felt this before? Why was one girl able to make him respond in a way no other girl had? There was something between them, a magic, a concern, a common understanding which had just happened, without origin, without effort, without development. It was just there. For the life of him, he could find no reason for it. In his mind he went over and over everything that had happened, each word, each expression, each meaning and movement and gesture. There was no explaining it. Something had happened between them which could not be calculated or reasoned. This puzzled him completely and made him feel slightly uneasy. It defied reason, and he could not trust it completely, but it was wonderful.

Sometimes, in the following days, he would be standing on the float alone, and the thought of Ellen Case would seize him and he would fling his arms out and jump and shout for joy, causing several sailboats in the harbor to jibe. The sailors could not figure what he was yelling about. He was happy, and he could not hold it in. His discipline suffered severe damage. He could not concentrate on anything, much less stand still, and sometimes being defeated by a perfectly simple operation, such as untying a knot, he felt rather silly. He was all thumbs. Immediately after eating he would be ravishingly hungry again, and, although he had always ignored hunger before he could not resist going to the snack bar and eating a hot dog each time the thought occurred to him. With horror he noticed he had gained two pounds in three weeks and imagined bulges of fat and shortness of breath. Ellen had given him a sense of security. He knew she would find him attractive even if he were overweight, and, for the first time, such a consideration mattered to him. He had never cared what people thought of him, and he really did not care now. But he cared what Ellen thought. He would hate to have her think poorly of him. The thought that she must ultimately do so depressed him no end.

How could he ever tell Ellen Case what he had done

to her? She hated someone named Tom Betancourt; she had to hate him, for the most basic reasons. And this selfsame Betancourt had come to her under a different name and caused her to love him. In doing so, he had not dispelled her hatred, had not replaced it with love; he had merely set love up in conflict with her hatred. How could he now make matters right?

He lay awake nights, worrying about it. He wanted to be honest with her. He knew he would have to tell her some time, and the longer he put it off the harder it her sometime, and the longer he put it off the harder it Never in his life had he feared anything, but that was simply because he had always been able to analyze things to exhaustion, ruling out all the unknowns and dealing only with facts. Here he was in a situation where everything was unknown; it was all a mystery. What would her reaction be? Would she be able to forgive him? He simply could not guess. She had been able to understand other things; perhaps she could understand this, too. Suddenly, Tom saw himself as a villain. And the vision made him sick.

They saw each other almost every day and spent most of the evenings together. Every free day Tom had they went sailing together in her blue one-ten, sometimes packing a lunch and landing on a distant beach to picnic. She scolded him the first time they sailed. A fresh breeze was blowing, and he had started off as if he were in a race. He close-hauled and heeled the boat over, sending them both up onto the gunwales, but taking very little water. He sailed perfectly, making the boat move through the water as fast as possible, and scared her half to death. She lectured him sternly, telling him to ease off or take her back to the Club. She was having none of it. Somewhat chagrined, he sat the boat down in the water and luffed all the way across the harbor. He found her a little hard to understand, at times.

He had been quite right in thinking she knew her way around a tennis court. They played frequently at dusk, when Tom's duties at the Club were over, and the courts were not being used. It was cool at that hour and they played with a passion. He thought she had a wonderful serve, for a woman, and was remarkably quick and cunning on the return. She was almost as good as his teammates at the University. He was delighted, because he had not had a good match in months, and it was his favorite sport. She was good enough to provide him with real exercise, and she was not about to lose to him, if she could help it. For the first time in his life, Tom lost his integrity, and he enjoyed doing it. He let her win. He laughed out loud when he saw how glad she was, and he chuckled everytime she crowed over it. He kept himself at her pace, which was not too much slower than his, and they had a fierce competition. Before Tom knew it, he found himself losing without intention. They would play long after it had become dark, rallying back and forth, not really being able to see the ball, Chuck yelling at them from the sidelines that they were both as mad as hatters. They enjoyed it immensely.

They never missed a film at the Yarmouth theatre, and Tom had to give up popcorn or grow sick of it. It did not matter if it was a western or a detective or something first-rate. They went to it, holding hands, eating candy and enjoying it. Afterwards, walking to the soda shop or driving out to the beach, they would discuss whatever film they had seen with a mock seriousness, comparing all westerns with *Othello* and all detectives with *Macbeth*. Once in a while they truly respected something they saw, and they would talk about it enthusiastically, giving points to each other's criticisms. Sometimes, in the evenings, they would just sit on the float or around the pool with Chuck and whatever young people would be around, drinking soft drinks and talking about people and ideas and things. Chuck was never able to keep up. He always spoke of religion, politics and other burning questions with the same understanding most people reserve for baseball. Perhaps he was right, and these discussions should never be treated in any other way. But he found himself over his head with Tom and Ellen. He marveled at Tom. In those discussions they had had before the season opened, Chuck was sure Tom had discussed things as enthusiastically as he, and from the same perspective. He could not understand how Tom could suddenly shift into high gear, leaving Chuck far behind him. Chuck felt a little resentful at Tom, but he was quick to get over it. Tom may have been bright, but he was a nice guy, too. Or some nights Tom and Ellen would drive to another beach and be by themselves. She spoke of her family a lot to him, trying to treat them fairly, but still, cutting into them fairly deep. She knew she was safe in saying these things to Tom; he would never repeat them. She often mentioned her brother's death. The two of them criticized the whole world, Tom more or less listening silently. He did not speak much about his own past. He wanted to, terribly, but he could never bring himself to it. He wanted to tell Ellen everything, have it spoken, see if it made sense, but he did not have the courage to do so. There was just too much to say. He would always bring her home at a reasonable hour, seldom meeting the elder Cases. When they were at home he only stayed a moment. He was always bored by the drink and the uneasy conversation.

For the first time, Tom really missed Casey. He

wanted to write him a letter, telling him the wonderful time he was having, not hesitating to speak his deepest thoughts and dreams to him. Neither of them had ever written much, their letters home being perfunctory to say the least. But sometimes during the summers they would write each other, discussing whatever was uppermost in their minds. They had no secrets from each other, not through any plan or arrangement, but simply because proximity in those years leaves little unsaid. They had always relied upon each other and could talk to each other endlessly on things they would not say to others. Tom wanted to tell someone about it all. He wanted to write the fact that he had found Ellen Case and thought her wonderful and was happier than he had ever been; he wanted to tell some long-standing and trusted friend that he suddenly envisioned himself as a villain and did not quite understand how it came to be. It did not make sense, and he could not get it to make sense: Ellen was Casey's sister; the boy they talked about in the car at night called Mac was actually Casey; the villain was Tom Betancourt, and Tom Betancourt was himself. And she loved him. He knew that. Tom wanted terribly to tell someone about it to see if he could not force it all to make sense.

He tried to make sense out of Casey's suicide as well, but without any success. He thought he might be able to know more about it now that he knew Ellen and the Cases, but he found himself going around in circles. He was not sure as yet how the Cases were different from his own family, or how Casey was different from him. He had let Ellen talk about it a lot. He could understand Casey's suicide now no better than before. He found himself off on an unexpected tangent. He was in love with Ellen Case, which he had never thought possible, and he was trying to adjust Casey's death from her point of view rather than from

159

his own. All his efforts failed. He knew what Chuck thought of it from a distance, and he knew what Ellen was beginning to think of it, but for his own sake, he could find no reason for believing such a thing. The evidence was not there to justify such a conclusion. Even if it were the truth, he could not see how it mattered. He was sorry Casey was dead, and he had been from the beginning. He missed him. But he could not make any sense of the death.

Finally, on a warm August night, he picked her up at her house. He was quiet, and he knew he looked a little sick. His face had a whiteness in it and his eyes were troubled and he did not react immediately when she spoke to him. He had decided he must tell her.

In the car, she said, "Where are we going?"

She was dressed in a bright skirt and knew there was a new film in the village.

"To the beach," he said.

"Right now?"

He did not answer so she took his free hand and watched him drive down the sandy road.

"All right," she said.

He knew his seriousness had scared her. He could tell from her face and her compliance that she was preparing herself to be told something. He wondered what she thought the bad news would be; probably some thing, such as his flunking school, or being drafted. He had never spoken of school to her. Or perhaps she was thinking of a bigger thing, such as some real reason why they could not be married. He had never spoken to her of his family either, and there could be a blotch there that would prevent a wise marriage. He knew she could have no inkling of what he did have to tell her. She was waiting patiently to be told.

At the beach, Tom pulled up and turned off the lights and, freeing his hand, lit a cigarette. She had never seen him smoke before. He leaned against his door, and she watched his face. Whatever he had to say was difficult for him.

"Ellen," he said. "I love you."

His voice was quaking and he was breathing deeply on the cigarette.

"I want to say that before anything else," he said. "I love you. I have never said that to anyone else, and I have never felt it. I love you very, very much."

She knew he meant it.

"I'm awfully glad."

She lay on her side, putting her hands and face on his hand, which was wide spread on the seat.

"But I have something terrible to tell you."

The suspense was wearing on her.

He said, slowly, carefully, "My name is Thomas Mathew Betancourt."

He felt her body jerk slightly, and her eyes open.

"Of course," she said, easily. "You're Mac's friend."

Then she sprang into a sitting position as the full impact of what this meant hit her.

"Oh, my God! You're Tom Betancourt!"

Her eyes were wide with horror as she looked at him across the dark seat and her mouth had fallen open.

She opened the door and got out and, stumbling, walked down the beach. She looked and acted as if she had received a physical blow. Through the windshield of the car, Tom thought she looked like a person going somewhere to vomit. She sat on the sand.

Tom went to her, kneeling in front of her, trying to take her head in his hands. Her face was wet with tears and she was sobbing.

"Can you forgive me," he asked. "Ellen? Can you ever understand and forgive me."

She pushed herself away from him.

161

She was on her knees, leaning over, crying into her hands. "I can't believe it," she said. "I can't believe it."

He sat cross-legged in the sand, listening to her crying, watching her body slump onto the sand, contract, writhe slightly. He could feel the spirit drain out of him. He could think of nothing to do or say that might make things better. He felt her shock and knew her tragedy and knew he was to blame and he felt very ashamed. Hearing her sobbing, he bit his tongue and wished he could feel some great pain which might make things better. He would rather die than have her be so hurt.

Finally she stood up and slowly climbed the beach back to the car.

She was sitting in the car with the door closed before he got up to follow her.

"Will you take me home?" she asked.

Her voice was the cracked and pitiful voice of a small girl. It tore his heart with sharp nails. He turned on the ignition and started the car and drove very slowly along the sandy road, trembling in the fear he might never see her again.

"Why did you do this, Tom? Why did you come here and make me fall in love with you? What could have possessed you?"

Her voice was shaking, and he was having difficulty finding the dark road.

"Honestly, I had no idea this would happen. Please believe me. I love you."

They drove in silence, Ellen weeping and Tom wishing he were dead.

At the house, he said, "Do you think you might ever be able to forgive me?"

She opened the door and put one foot on the ground.

162

"I might be able to forgive you, Tom. But if I did, I would never be able to live with myself."

He sat in the car, watching her go into the house. And then he drove back to the beach. He wanted to smash something, to hear glass break and steel tear. No matter what he did, he could not control his breathing and he could not control his emotion. He held his breath, but still the tears came. Biting his lips did no good; he sobbed, letting his breath out in a stream which made his whole body quiver. At the beach he ran to the water, flinging off his clothes and throwing himself in, diving clumsily and splashing for some moments before he got into the rhythm of his stroke. He swam far out into the water and finally floated on his back, gasping for breath. He had a mild cramp in his stomach and the pain thrilled him. The first moment he had breath he dove as far under water as he could and swallowed water coming up. He saw stars and waited a moment, lying calmly in the water, moving enough to keep him afloat. Slowly, then, he swam ashore.

He was exhausted. He fell on the sand, lay on his stomach and cried. It had been a long time since he had cried and he had forgotten the taste of it and the exhaustion of it. He ground his face into the sand so that it cut him, and he cried to himself, "Oh God, oh God, oh God."

Fifteen

The next morning Tom felt half dead. Despite Chuck's uncomprehending coercion, he simply could not get out of bed. It was his day off anyway, so it did not really matter. He told Chuck he was not feeling well and asked him to be quiet. Chuck finally went away. For hours Tom lay in his bed looking at the cracked plainboard ceiling of his shack, not moving and hardly blinking. He felt exhausted. Frequently before he had felt tired from sports or studying but it was always a pleasant, sleepy sort of tiredness which did not dampen his enthusiasm. He had never felt so limp and suddenly dead. He thought it might be his soul that was tired, the feeling ran so deep and was so thorough.

He spent the whole morning in his room, dressed in his shorts. He paced up and down, looking out the window at the sea, listening to the noises of the children playing by the pool. It grew hot and he found himself sweating profusely. Once or twice he tried to do pushups but was only able to manage a few. He had no enthusiasm and could not concentrate on doing them. He picked up a book, a novel by Steinbeck, and stretched out on the bed, tried reading it, but it did not hold his attention. He smoked, but it only made him feel hotter. Finally, near noon, the heat drove him into the shower and he changed into his shirt and slacks.

He came back to the Club, after driving to the

village for a sandwich. An idea had occurred to him. He knew his calling the Case house and asking for Ellen would be useless. Doubtless, in her shock and near hysteria, she had told her parents who Tom Mathews was, and they would certainly have put her beyond further contact with him. They would never let her speak to him, and it was doubtful whether she herself would want to anyway. His call, or his going there, would not be welcome. Either would be fruitless. But he had to know if she was all right, if she was taking it well or if she had harmed herself. He imagined all sorts of things she might do. Again, he had to put the thought of Casey's action from his mind. He knew that if Chuck called, she would know it was really Tom calling. And it might mean nothing to her.

Chuck was agreeable, as Tom knew he would be. Chuck did not ask any questions but limited his comment to the statement that there were plenty of beans in the pot and placed the call, asking for Ellen. He was told Ellen had gone to Philadelphia to visit some school friends and would be back in two weeks.

Of course Tom knew she had not gone. She might have, but if she felt anything like the way he did, she would not want to go anywhere. He rather thought she was moping around the house, feeling as bad as he, wanting time to think things over. He assumed there was a hint in the statement. She would need at least two weeks to think things over, and then perhaps she would see him. How would he ever live through the two weeks.

For all the self-discipline Tom had, now he was a shambles. He performed his duties at the Club listlessly and without thinking. The children to whom he had been teaching sailing all summer saw the change in him and played havoc. It was impossible to keep them in their life preservers, and they hurled each other off the float with great glee. Always before, this had been expressly forbidden. Tom could not keep his mind on them. He moved from here to there as if in a daze, barely hearing a word anyone said to him. A party would come into their mooring from boating and halloo at him again and again but he would not hear them, or move to pick them up until someone at the Club came down to tell him to move. He would sit, whenever left alone, and stare into space. He would stand for hours at the edge of the float looking into the water, watching the Tommy Cods but not really seeing them. He simply could not think.

After a few days of this, Chuck took mercy on him and took him to play tennis at dusk. He was no good at it, and knew it, but he whooped and hollered around as if it were great fun. He was a dismal failure. Tom swung at the ball halfheartedly, not caring if it went into the net or not. Soon they gave up in the middle of a game and Chuck followed Tom into his shack with a bottle of beer. They sat and drank it, Chuck trying to be chummy and Tom trying to be polite. Chuck had no ability to make people talk, and this became apparent to him shortly after midnight. He left Tom and went to bed, knowing no more than when he had started, hours earlier.

Most nights, Tom drove around in his car. He would get onto Route 6, a speedway, and drive to Province-town New Beach without going into the town and then drive back again. He would have his suppers in the village, ignoring the people who came in and went out. He seldom spoke to anyone and when someone spoke to him he frequently did not hear what was said. People noticed he was completely unable even to appear friendly and they remembered the incident with the dog and thought that he must be sensitive after all.

He did not care about them; for the most part, he shunned people.

As the two week period was drawing to a close, he developed a curious shiver that went through his whole body. He would find himself sitting on the float shaking like a puppy. He could not stop it. His legs would be stretched out before him on the planks and he would see his knees shaking and feel it in his hips and shoulders. He would wrap his arms around himself like a small boy and for a moment it would stop, only to start again. He would make himself busy with something but immediately lose interest in it. Each time he stood or sat still he would shake. He felt cold.

Thinking did little good. He tried to prepare himself for the worst, laying out all emotions and personalities and involvements in his lap before him, analyzing them and calculating the importance of each element. He thought of the Cases and tried to understand them in the light of his own family. The two families had much in common, but somewhere there was a tremendous difference. He thought of his own father, the senior Betancourt, realizing the man led a distinct and separate way of life. He had not depended too much upon his family but had thrown himself into his own affairs with enthusiasm and success. He did not need his wife or son, and had never professed to. Tom marveled at the clarity of his father's thinking. He thought Mr. Case must be different. Case was a wealthy man, too, and did not have to practice as an architect. Tom guessed from what Ellen had said that he had never really thrown himself into it. He was forever moving about the world, from Florida to Cannes, with his wife and members of his family, being constantly distracted from them, but never enough. He had been more distracted from his work. Not working very hard at anything, he had been chiefly dependent upon his family.

Tom guessed from things Ellen had said that the family had collided more than once. There had been dreadful scenes. Tom could not remember there ever having been an angry scene in his own family.

Mrs. Case was quite different from his mother, too. She had none of his mother's stability. He knew from the way she had approached him at the Club that she must be forever off having silly little, half-drunken affairs which afforded her no particular satisfaction. They would distract her, perhaps, but she would always be thrust back upon her family. His mother had never done that. She had been having a satisfactory affair for more than eight years, and she had never had to look to her family for support. Thinking about this, Tom wrinkled his brow in consternation. He was not sure one arrangement was better than the other. His family lived together, more or less, but they meant nothing to each other and they all knew it. They never looked to each other for support of any sort. Each member was self-contained. The Cases, on the other hand, lived together but were always looking to each other for support. It had been a tense cohesion, with many collisions. There had been bitter fights, and, of course, much lack of self-discipline, and, much out-of-hand drinking. Were they trying to assuage their guilt by rubbing against each other? Tom was sure they were hampered by a sense of sin which drove them endlessly into each other. He was not sure the resulting cohesion of the family was at all good. There was a difference in the families, but it was beyond Tom to guess which was the better.

He let another half week go by, giving Ellen more time than he had presumed she requested to think things over. His thinking about the Cases had done some good. He had come to the conclusion that their own sense of guilt over Casey's death had driven them toward each other again, making them even more of a unit. The proof of this, in Tom's mind, was that Ellen had thought it necessary to spend the summer with her parents. He knew there had been friction all summer. He knew that if Ellen's involvement with Tom Betancourt were thrown at the family, as it most likely was, they would become even a tighter unit and his hope would be lost. He would know the minute he saw them. Ellen had the job of either acting like a Case, returning to her parents and rubbing against them, or acting like someone else, possibly a Betancourt, and standing free. Tom was not sure which would be better. Certainly when she had been talking about her family, cutting into them, she had spoken like someone standing free. But Tom knew families were odd things, having unique powers and incalculable force. Tom knew Ellen would need all the time he could give her.

Finally he could put it off no longer. He was not eating or sleeping or getting any exercise and he knew he would become sick if he did not get hold of himself. For the first time, his effort of cold analysis had left a rawness in his mind and a bad taste in his mouth. He had been barely able to make himself think about the Cases. But he knew he had to, even if he were not able to control his emotions while doing so. He was shivering constantly. He was sick to death of everything and could stand it no longer. One evening at dusk he drove to the Case house.

The house looked cold and gray and barren as he approached it. There was a strong wind blowing across the peninsula from the east and it was blowing rain and spray with it. The salt was clogging his windshield wipers. They were barely working, creeping back and forth across the glass. The road was mud.

He stopped the car in front of the house and ran for

the front door so as to not get wet. The horsefaced servant opened it to him and allowed him in with some hesitation. She was not smiling.

Tom turned the corner inside the house and went up the stairs to the living room. He could sense, almost see, the Cases waiting for him. He pictured them huddled around the fireplace, sitting close to each other, looking towards the door. He entered the living room, standing at one end. His picture of how they would be had been exact. The picture he had of them in his head shifted perfectly into reality. There they were before him. Ellen and her mother were sitting on the divan in front of the fireplace, close together, Ellen nearer the fireplace. Mr. Case was sitting in a chair across from them, his back to the door. His bald spot, over the back of the chair, reflected light. There were demitasses about. The three looked lost in the big room, sitting around the enormous, cold fireplace. There was light from only one floor lamp. They all turned to look at Tom. His heart sank.

Tom had the feeling he was about to go through a strange, human ritual, one of ultimate rejection. He was not sure what it would be like, but at first he thought, in order to make it full and complete, he would have to go through it for them. He knew instinctively, looking at them, his cause was lost. But he felt that staying, letting their emotion spew all over him would be helping them in some way. He was sure there would be the usual, predictable, unrestrained emotion splashed at him, with vehemence. He prepared himself for the role he would have to play in this scene. Then he wondered, momentarily, how much he was doing this for himself. There was something he had to expunge as well. Anyway, it was going to happen.

Case pushed himself out of his chair, violently.

"Good God, what are you doing here?"

"I came to see if Ellen were all right," Tom said.

He went forward, half way across the room, and stopped. He had been in the shadows of the far end of the room.

Ellen and her mother were looking at him from the divan. Mrs. Case snaked her hand out, putting it on Ellen's hand, in a gesture of protection. Ellen closed her eyes and put her head down.

Case shouted, "Ellen certainly does not want to see you."

Tom was trying to see Ellen's face. She looked tired and white and drawn. She was dressed in a blue wool sweater and skirt.

"That's for Ellen to say," Tom said.

"I'm telling you," Case said, sternly. "Ellen does not want to see you, and you are to get out of here at once."

Tom saw the flash of real anger in his eyes and he was mildly surprised. The man hitched up his pants with his thumbs. For once, Case did not seem drunk. He seemed almost capable.

"What a rotten boy you are," Mrs. Case said.

She was stroking Ellen's hand in a manner almost maternal. Tom thought even she felt utterly protected with Case standing between them.

"At once," Case said, quietly.

Tom said, "Ellen?"

She raised her head. He could see the reflection of light from her eyes and knew they were flooded with tears.

"Go away, Tom. I don't want to ever see you. Ever again."

She said the words slowly and with difficulty, not wanting to sob. Each one thudded deep in Tom's inside. He had expected it, but still, he could not take it. He was unable to move. His eyes watered and his

171

mouth opened and he could not speak. The room had become filmy through his tears. He stood, shocked and dumb.

Now that the ritual was over, there was a terrible scene. It was obvious to all that Tom was crying, that he was beaten, that he was weak before them. Before he knew it, Case had sprung at him, grabbing him, hitting him, shouting, and pushing him toward the stairs that led down to the door. All that he was shouting did not make sense to Tom and Tom put his hands out to protect himself but he could not see so he put his arms over his face. He heard Mrs. Case screaming and knew he was being hit repeatedly and clumsily and that he was moving backwards towards the door to the stairwell. Finally, he was able to see Mrs. Case and Ellen standing near the fireplace, arms around each other, and heard Ellen screaming.

"Please go, Tom! Please go!"

He turned and found the stairs and ran down them and out the door.

He sat in his car, clenching his hands together and shaking. He could not collect himself. Through the rain-streaked windshield he saw the door of the house open and the large frame of Case standing in the rectangle of light, pointing something at him. Tom thought he was pointing his hand. Suddenly there was an explosion. Case was standing in the doorway deliberately shooting at him. Tom glanced at the windshield and saw it was cracked. Quickly he turned the key of the ignition and started the car. His wheels spun in the mud, but he took his foot off the accelerator and pressed down more lightly and the car bolted out of the mud, slipping sideways. He heard two more explosions but he never thought to duck. The car was swerving and he could barely control it.

He came to the public road and leapt onto it; the car

continued to skid and swerve. He was far from the house now but he pressed the accelerator to the floor. The engine roared and he saw the raindrops coming at the car with amazing speed. The windshield wipers were working slowly and he knew he was not seeing enough. He skidded on the curve and tried to slow the car down. He remembered the speed limit on this old wood road was twenty-five, but he felt he was going slowly when the speedometer read forty-five. Going across open places the wind pushed against the car, making it swerve further, and the wheel felt very light in his hands.

He had to get control of himself and he knew it. He was crying and the windshield was wet and he could not see. He heard himself sobbing and he thought it a strange noise but he could not stop it. The fleeting thought crossed his mind that he was going to have an accident and he wondered if it was a premonition. He must not have an accident. He jammed on his brakes on a curve at the last possible moment, barely making it, and stepped on the accelerator again. He must slow down. All the good years of caution and discipline spoke to him in a quiet voice: you must slow down; you must be careful; you know you cannot do this without having an accident; you must slow down. Sobbing, he careened on through the night, the car feeling light in his hands, the road slippery. He marveled at his ability to govern the car, seeing that he could barely see. Years of keeping himself in top condition, of developing the fastest reflexes, kept him from smashing up on several curves. Each one he would barely pull out of, speeding again while the car was still swaying and out of complete control. He yelled something at himself and did not care what he was saying. It was just a voice, another voice in a long line of voices. He did not care. He drove onto the bridge, watching the

173

ghostly, hard, white cement railing speeding past him, blurring, and he knew he was close to scraping it. The car heaved as it came off the bridge and Tom felt his front right wheel hit sand and with horror he saw that he was going seventy-five miles an hour. The steering wheel spun on him as the front wheels buckled in the sand and he felt the rear of the car come up behind him. He threw himself onto the seat beside him, but at the same time he was thrown into the air as the car began to turn over. For a moment he thought he was being thrown free of the car. He felt his neck crash into the metal roof support and he heard the canvas rip. Then slowly he saw the edge of the car coming down on top of him and he realized he was incredibly balanced on the top of the windshield, half through the canvas, and the car was rolling completely over and would land on top of him. He saw the fenders and side of the car bearing down on him like an avalanche and he could not understand why it was coming so slowly. It was the slowest moving thing he had ever seen. He flung his hands out, gripping pieces of torn canvas, trying to pull his weight against them. He heard the crash of steel against the ground and pictured the flat of the hood falling down the extra foot or two.

He felt blood in his mouth and could taste it. It was welling up and he knew it was liable to choke him. He swallowed as much as he could and snorted to clear his nose.

His head was outside the car and looking straight up he could see the clean, yellow door and, on either side above him, the wheels. The rear wheels were still turning and they made a nice, rhythmical noise. He had lost track of where his hands had gone but he imagined they were somewhere under the car. His legs and feet were rather numb but he could feel something pressing against his right knee. Tremendous amounts of blood were coming into his mouth and he tried spitting it out but it ran down his cheeks. He could not move.

In a short while the wheels stopped spinning and the rhythmical noise stopped. The rain was falling on his upturned face and he could not close his eyes against it. He could hear and smell the car burning and once or twice he caught a sight of the flame as a tongue of it lashed out from above him and was blown sideways in the wind. It was hopeless. The road was seldom used and no one would have heard the crash. Eventually someone might see the fire, but it would be too late. Even if a rescue squad should arrive at the moment, they would not be able to do anything. They would not have time to free him before the car exploded. It was hopeless.

He had always known emotion would kill him, his own or somebody else's. The fact that this emotion turned out to be love, he did not find too surprising.

You're cool Fletch. You're witty, sophisticated, and completely irresistible. Your new assignment is to track down a multimillion-dollar art heist.

But there's this lovely dead blonde in your apartment, and all the evidence points to only one person...

And you don't think you did it. The police think otherwise, so you'd better find the murderer yourself, or else...

GREGORY MCDONALD
Author of FLETCH

30882/$1.75   FESS 11-76